# THE TOLL

## OF

# BEING THE LITTLE

# MAN

# R.K.SMITH

The Toll of Being the Little Man

By R.K. Smith

**Copyright © 2020 by R.K. Smith**

Printed in the United States of America

First Printing, 2020

10 9 8 7 6 5 4 3 2 1

ISBN ebook 978-1-7351865-1-1

ISBN Paperback 978-1-7351865-0-4

# TABLE OF CONTENTS

# INTRODUCTION

The story that was told by my uncle Daniel, started with the capturing of black men against their will and bringing them to the western shores for economic purposes. The process of slavery continued to separate fathers from their families, creating a lasting impression. Once freedom was finally obtained, and free will was put to practice, economic injustices and other factors sometimes prevented the commitment to fatherhood from being established in the generations that followed. When circumstances within the family dynamics became unbearable, many fathers would often leave.

The common absence of the father in the home birthed what is known as "The Little Man." Birth order does not determine who will become the little man of the household. Sometimes, the oldest son is chosen and sometimes a younger son is reared into the role, as the mother identifies qualities of assuming responsibility and loyalty in his personality at an early age. The role of the "Little Man" consists of stepping into the responsibility of fatherhood and husbandry while still a young boy. The task of being the provider and protector will continue throughout his adolescence age. The burden of this responsibility disrupts the child's ability to function as a man later in adulthood, causing him to err when it comes to becoming a productive husband and father in his own household. These young boys often grow up to become confused men when deciphering who comes first; their mother or their wife; their own children or their grown-up siblings. Preexposure to adulthood in some cases creates the foundation for a continuous cycle of broken families as the little boy - trapped inside the man, seeks the less stressed, adventurous childhood he has been denied.

The relationship between the son and mother, who plays the restricted role of the surrogate wife is established throughout childhood. Mental anguish on behalf of the son comes into play when the mother continues to step outside that role, having several relationships with different men to accommodate the intimate needs that her son cannot fulfill. The son is left broken, confused, and humiliated by his diminishing title in the presence of his mother's significant other. Since the mother is the first example the "Little Man" sees of the opposite sex, the lens for which he views women becomes tainted with the same distrust and animosity that he has developed towards his mother over time. When manipulation, abuse, and the faintest amount of relational inappropriateness have crept into the relationship, the young man is riddled with shame and guilt and remains in psychological turmoil, usually preventing any possibility of having a wholesome relationship with any other woman and his views are distorted when it comes to rearing his own children.

# ME AND THE GUYS

M y name is Timothy, I consider myself to be a fairly, attractive looking guy. One thing I did not inherit from my father's side of the gene pool is height, I'm about 5 ft 8', but it works for me. I am a firm believer in working hard and saving as much money as possible. I enjoy running, watching football, and following politics whenever I have the time. Unlike my friends, I'm not a socialite, I consider myself to be a deep thinker, I worry and stress a lot which could all be avoided if I ever learn to say "No." After completing 5 years in the Army, and a few jobs in-between, I went back to school to become a Commercial Industrial Plumber. My signature is all over most of the new infrastructure in downtown Birmingham. I pride myself in my appearance, as I have a keen eye for fashion, but my conservative instincts tend to guide me towards the clearance rack. I have over 40 boxes of unworn shoes, 10 stylish jackets, and countless new garments that are at least fifteen years old. I work so much that I seldom get to enjoy the fruits of my labor. My friend, Jake teases me that the Salvation Army doesn't even want my clothes because they are so outdated, but I have a hard time parting with anything. When I'm not catching up on my laundry, I'm usually cleaning my new silver extended cab Dodge, Ram. I usually take it for a drive on the weekends, but I mostly drive my work truck, to and from work.

Jake is tall, muscular, and light-skinned. He's a pretty good guy, yet annoyingly opinionated and cheaper than me. Jake drives an old brown Ford pickup and his house is paid for, which affords him to live comfortably, and put most of his money in a savings account. Jake works for U.S. Locomotives. He usually works 10-12 hours a day, and as much overtime as he can on the weekends. Jake earns a lot more than the average blue-collar worker, but the impressions of his impoverished childhood plague him to believe that he can never have enough money. When Jake was single, he bought his groceries and supplies in bulk - at the local Costco. Every Fall, he would alternate between purchasing a cow or a hog from the local farmer and he would have everything prepped into steaks, sausage, tenderloin, and ground beef or pork. Living on 10 acres of land with a large lake, Jake utilizes his land for hunting deer, rabbits, squirrels, and going fishing whenever he could. In his deep freezer, he had enough meat to last a year. Driving by Jake's house in the early summer, you can't help but be mesmerized by a beautiful garden of turnip greens, field peas, corn, tomatoes, okra, and peppers of different sorts.

Prior to Jake's marriage, he could never resist the opportunity for an innocent moment to flirt. His masculine disposition, and good looks, disguises his previous perception of women. Whenever Jake gets a day off, he loves to stroll into the bank and ask the teller for an account balance. Jake enjoys watching the expression on her face when she sees how much money is in his account. As the teller looks up at Jake to hand him his receipt, he gently grabs the slender sheet of paper from her hands and places it inside his wallet. "Is there anything else I can help you with Mr. Jones?" she asks. It gives Jake all the pleasure in the world to smile at the teller and say, "No, that will be all." When Jake turns and walks away, he knows the teller's eyes are tracking his every step. For most of his life, Jake believed that all women were impressed with men who have a lot of money.

Our other running buddy is Matt. He's tall, slim, and dark-skinned with silver and black wavy hair, a very neat and clean-cut guy. Matt's hair started turning gray in his twenties. He's the Pastor of Meadow Brook Holiness/Pentecostal Church, which was on its way to becoming the first Megachurch in Meadow Brook. Matt is married to Phoebe and they have three grown children. Matt has won countless numbers of souls for Christ, whether they were church attendees or random people on the streets. He has advised many politicians and government officials in the city of Meadow Brook during his time as a pastor. Matt was a Supervisor at the Vintage Oats, Cereal Company but when the church started to grow, he began to earn a significant wage, allowing him to leave the work force and pastor fulltime. Matt was able to provide a comfortable lifestyle for himself and his family to go on vacations, while he accumulated nice savings and retirement plans. With an unexpected turn of events at this stage in his life, Matt has had to return to work for one reason but he feels his presence is needed continuously at the church for many other reasons.

Things are looking better for myself and Jake now. Life has architecturally reshaped our ideologies and belief systems. As for Matt, due to his own twist of fate, he has his own purgatory to escape.

# 1

## (1965)

Long before me, my little brother Ron, and my little sister Cindy were born, my mom, who I call Lena, my grandmother, whom we all call Momma, Aunt Liz and Uncle Daniel lived together. Momma was a big lady. She was 5ft 10' tall and weighed about 250lbs, and she was not the kindest person to be around - at least not to her children and grandchildren. My grandfather was a short stocky-built farmer, who stood about 5ft 7' tall and weighed about 130lbs. He died when my mother was eight years old, leaving my grandmother with eight children. I think that was the root of her bitterness. My mother and her siblings were small in stature like their father. They feared my grandmother, and so did every generation afterward. Lena, Aunt Liz, and Uncle Daniel took good care of her, paying all the bills, giving her spending money, and waiting on her hand and foot. Momma was fifty years old and had no physical disabilities that would prevent her from working. She instilled an unrelenting fear in her children that it was their responsibility to take care of her and they were shamed if they ever thought about not doing so, as she had come to depend on them for everything. When her older children finished school or were old enough to leave home, they left and very seldom came back to visit, other than to see how their siblings were doing. Whoever was left at home, inherited the wrath of tending to her every need. Momma did as she pleased. She was an active member at Meadowbrook's First Baptist Church, she volunteered at a women's community group, she played Bingo on Friday nights and had lots of friends in the neighborhood. It seems like she would have been more content with her life, but she harbored a wave of anger that could not be relinquished.

Lena is the sixth child, she dropped out of school when she was 16 years old; along with her younger sister - to help take care of their mother. Now, Lena is 20, Aunt Liz is 17, and Uncle Daniel is 15 years old. My grandmother never worked while my grandfather was alive. After his demise, she lost the farm, and they had to move into Meadow Creek Apartments where they all live now.

Momma had her own room and so did Uncle Daniel. Lena and Aunt Liz shared a room. Good paying jobs were scarce, especially if you didn't have an education. Lena worked as a janitor at Meadow Brook Hospital, Aunt Liz worked at Jolynn's Kitchen, cooking, and serving soul food. Since my uncle was still in high school, he worked at Jolynn's at night. With all three of their incomes, it was a struggle to pay the bills, take care of Momma, and keep food on the table. It didn't help that Momma was such a picky eater, she never noticed the struggles of her children, and neither did she care. They never complained to her for fear of her physical retaliation.

# 2

## THE SNOWSTORM

It was the middle of January, and the local news broadcast had been reporting that a snowstorm was headed towards Meadowbrook. That Monday night, the snow began to accumulate. When Momma, Lena, and Aunt Liz woke up the next morning, snow was all over the ground. It was cold in the apartment, the power was out due to the settling of the snow on the power lines, and there was hardly anything to eat. Momma complained that she needed something to eat because of her diabetes. Lena was the oldest, and she knew she had to think fast, so she got up and walked over to the closet to grab her hat, scarf, and coat. "Where are you going Lena?" asked Aunt Liz. "Somebody has to go," replied Lena. Aunt Liz walked over to Lena and whispered, "You don't have any money, we just scraped up enough money to pay the bills and plus, you don't know how bad it is outside." "What if you freeze out there and don't make it back?" "I'll be okay, I'll think of something." "Just stay here with Momma and I'll be back as soon as possible." Lena bundled up and she left out of the front door, being very careful not to slip and fall on the frozen steps. She noticed that the sun was beaming, which was a good sign, maybe the snow would start to melt soon, she thought. When Lena closed the door, Uncle Daniel woke up. He got out of the bed and came in the front room wearing his pajamas and draped in a blanket. "Where is Lena, he asked?" She insisted on going out in the snow by herself to get Momma something to eat. Uncle Daniel replied, "Why didn't anyone wake me?" "I could have gone with her." "We heard you come in from work late last night before the snowstorm got worse and we knew you needed to rest, that's why we didn't bother you." Uncle Daniel, Aunt Liz, and Momma sat by the window, wrapped in blankets - waiting for Lena to return.

Lena had been thinking about how they were going to get food in the house all night but waking up to the snowstorm made the situation much worse. Winded and shivering, Lena tread the snow that stood 2-feet, one step at a time. Finally, she arrived at Sam's Stop-N-Shop about an hour after she left the apartment. Ordinarily, it would have taken about twenty minutes to get there. The parking lot had been shoveled but it was still slippery in spots. Fortunately, that part of town had power and since Sam lived right behind his store, he only had to walk over and open it up. The store was run by his wife, his teenage son, and daughter, and a couple of school kids would bag groceries on normal afternoons. When Lena arrived at the door, she stomped the snow off her shoes outside, adjusted her coat and scarf, and walked over to the young man sweeping the floor, who was Sam's son. Lena took a deep breath and asked to speak to Sam. The young man didn't say anything, he just looked at her for a few seconds, propped his broom against the wall, and went to the back of the store to find his father. Lena didn't know how this was going to turn out. In the past, her father had shared stories with her and her siblings about his father having to ask for favors as a tenant farmer. The repayment was always unfair or almost unpayable. Therefore, she certainly wasn't comfortable having to ask someone outside her race for hand-outs, but she had no other choice.

Sam was a tall, burly looking guy, in his mid-fifties, but he was reasonable. As he made his way to the front of the store where Lena was standing, the only thing she could focus on was the lines on Sam's blue and white plaid shirt as he got closer. Sam stopped in front of Lena, wearing brown leather boots and wrangler jeans. He asked in a curious tone, "Did you want to see me?" Sam locked his legs and folded his arms. Lena took a deep swallow, straightened her back, and stuttered, "Yes, yes sir." "I know you don't know me personally, but my family has fallen on hard times, we don't have any food in the house and I was just wondering if you would trust me with a bag of cornmeal and a bag of flour on credit?" "I will pay you back at the end of the week." Sam looked at Lena, then he rubbed his fingers through his scruffy beard and looked down at the floor. After clearing his throat, he said, "This is not the way I usually conduct my business, but I'll do it this time."

"Follow me," he said. Lena was able to relax her shoulders now and she followed Sam to the back where the store office was. Once inside, Sam sat in the chair behind the desk and asked Lena what her first and last name was. He wrote it on a sheet of paper along with the calculated cost and tax of the cornmeal and flour. Sam wrote the same thing on another sheet of paper and handed it to Lena. He slid the other piece of paper that he kept for himself into his desk drawer. Sam got on the store intercom and asked for

Joni, his daughter - who was at register 1, to come with a bag of cornmeal and flour to his office. A few minutes later, Joni showed up looking suspicious and said, "Here you go dad," then, she returned to her register to restock the bags. Sam placed the flour and cornmeal in a used grocery bag that had been laying in the corner of his office and pushed them across the desk towards Lena. She grabbed the two bags and said, "Thank you so much, I promise I will pay you by the end of the week!" Lena got up and made her way back to the front of the store. It felt as though the walk through the store was longer than the walk to the store as Lena could feel Joni staring at her as she passed by her register and made her way to the door. Lena didn't look to see who else was watching, she just kept looking straight ahead with the cornmeal and flour clutched in her arms. Once Lena got outside, she scanned the parking lot, trying to remember which way she had previously traveled across, so she wouldn't fall on the slippery areas. After crossing the parking lot, Lena tread through the deep snow again as fast as her legs would carry her.

Back home, Aunt Liz and Uncle Daniel were starting to worry, Lena had been gone over two hours now. They kept looking out of the window to see if they could make out anything that possibly resembled her from a distance.

Momma just sat there complaining that she was hungry, and she wanted to know what was taking Lena so long.

When Lena arrived at Meadow Creek Apartments, she was surprised to see that the streetlight was back on and so were many of the lights in the apartment complex. She carefully climbed the steps and unlocked the door to their apartment and went inside. Aunt Liz was waiting at the door to help her with whatever she had gotten. "I could have gone with you Lena", said Uncle Daniel. "I knew you needed your rest," she said. Lena was busy taking off the layers and walking over to check the thermostat. Lena went to the refrigerator to see what was in it. There was a single stick of margarine and a little bit of milk left in a jug. In the freezer, was a family-size pack of pork neck bones and two full ice trays. Lena made fried cornbread cakes to go with the pot of neckbones. The first plate was made for Momma, then Lena and her siblings ate. By Wednesday evening, nothing was left but a pot of liquid from the neck bones. Lena continued to make fried cornbread to go with the broth and she made flour flapjacks without syrup for breakfast.

By Thursday, the snow had melted. After work on Friday evening, Lena went to cash her paycheck. When she placed the money in her coat-pocket, she felt something else rubbing against the back of her fingers. Lena thought maybe it was some old receipts, but when she pulled the papers out, it was 20 single dollar bills. She figured Uncle Daniel must have slipped his tip money from Jolynn's into her coat pocket for groceries the night before when he got in from work. He knew Lena was asleep, and he didn't want to wake her. Lena folded all the bills together, placed them back inside her coat pocket, and went to pay Sam for the cornmeal and flour. When Lena arrived at Sam's Stop N' Shop, Joni wasn't there but she wished she was, to show her that she was not only paying her debts but getting enough groceries to fill the entire refrigerator, even if it meant she would have to walk to work next week because she wouldn't have transportation fare.

Lena continued to work at the hospital during the day and eventually, she was able to get a part-time job working at Meadow Brook Middle School as a janitor at night. Momma didn't appreciate anything Lena did, she argued and fought with her every day - no matter how hard she worked.

# 3

## THE START OF
## SOMETHING NEW

What a long week, Lena thought. It was almost Friday and she was about to complete her first week of working two jobs. She wasn't looking forward to dealing with Momma's insults when she got home. Lena was getting tired of living the same old routine, never getting ahead, always working but never having anything to show for it. She wanted to go back to school but she knew that her family was depending on her and Momma had embedded into their heads that they were obligated to see that she was taken care of, any other way would be disgraceful. Lena was determined that Uncle Daniel was going to finish school, so he would have a better life someday. She felt in her heart that she would always be tied to her mother.

Lena's friend Kathy was a janitor at the middle school too. One night after work, Kathy met Lena near the steam room in the basement where they were putting their mops and brooms away. They became friends back in kindergarten. Kathy dropped out of high school because she had gotten pregnant, but she had more financial support at home than Lena. Both of her parents worked, and she just had to pay her younger sister for babysitting. "Girl, all you do is work," said Kathy. "The bills won't pay themselves," replied Lena. "How about you come to Bill's Place with me tonight?" "I don't know Kathy," Lena replied, "I'm already tired, you know I don't drink and besides, I got a lot of stuff to take care of early in the morning." "You don't have to drink, just come and socialize, you know... escape our miserable realities for a moment." Lena didn't say anything. "Oh, come on, you deserve a break." All Lena could think about was her mother at home and what she would say if she suspected she was hanging out late at some bar.

Lena reluctantly agreed to go with Kathy to Bill's Place for a few minutes. They pulled up in Kathy's red Pacer. Kathy looked at Lena and told her to lose the work apron. Lena folded her apron and laid it on Kathy's car seat, then she turned around and gazed at the silhouettes on the curtains of Bill's Place before they got to the door. Once inside, there was a haze of cigarette smoke, a mirror ball, and different colored lights spinning around the room. "Loosen up," said Kathy. "You are too tense, let's sit over here in the corner, at the round booth." It wasn't long before a guy came over to talk to Kathy, she never felt nervous about talking to guys or meeting a stranger, whereas Lena was busy scoping out the joint and every person inside. Several more guys came over to say hi to Kathy and eventually moved on. After sitting there for a few minutes, a guy came over to ask Kathy about Lena. Lena looked at the man from head to toe, then she looked away. He whispered something in Kathy's ear, she giggled, and he got up and walked away. "Who was that?" asked Lena. "You don't want to know," replied Kathy. "He's just up to no good as usual." Suddenly, the crowd seemed to disperse, making way for Lena to notice a guy at the bar having a drink. He was very attractive, but he looked kind of young. Once he laid eyes on Lena, he sat his shot glass down and made his way over to where she and Kathy were sitting. They both noticed him coming their way at the same time. "Look, girl, I think somebody's checking you out," said Kathy. Lena didn't know what she would say to him or what he would ask. "Just relax," said Kathy, slapping Lena on the thigh under the table. As the stranger approached their table, he greeted them by saying, "Hey ladies." They both looked up at him. "What's your name?" he asked Lena, "I never seen you in here before." Lena looked up at the handsome stranger and said, "My name is Lena, why?" Kathy nudged her in the side. "Excuse me, I meant, What's your name?" The stranger responded, "Timothy," but I go by Tim." "Nice to meet you, Ms. Lena." Lena looked at Kathy nervously and said, "It's getting late, we really should be going now." "Are you sure?" "We just got here." "I know, but I have to get up early in the morning to run some errands," she reminded Kathy. "Well alright," said Kathy, accepting that she had lost the argument, "I guess the party's over." As they slid from around the table, Tim said, "I certainly hope to see you again Ms. Lena." Kathy said bye to Tim, but Lena didn't say a word, she was too nervous. Lena was glad to meet Tim, but her anxiety took over and she was speechless. When they got outside, they giggled all the way to the car. Kathy said, "Girl, he sure was sweet on you!" "I told you, it wasn't that bad now - was it?" "No, but I got to get home." Kathy remembered Lena telling her about her mother when they were children, but she thought for sure, her mother would have mellowed out by now, especially since Lena was 20 years old.

Kathy dropped Lena off at her apartment and waited until she got inside and turned the porch light off. Kathy put the car in reverse so she could turn around and exit the complex. Once Lena was inside, the apartment was silent and completely dark. When she turned the light on, Momma had been sitting on the sofa in the dark - waiting to be the first thing Lena saw so that she wouldn't have time to come up with an excuse for being out late at night. Lena was so startled as she stood there with her right hand over her chest. Lena's heartbeat started to increase as the sofa creaked when Momma lifted her weight off it. "So, where have you been?" Momma asked, walking in Lena's direction. "Momma, you startled me," said Lena, trying to think of something to say. "I bet I did," said Momma. "So, you think you're supposed to be hanging out late at night now?" "No mam, Kathy just invited me to her house for a little while," Lena lied. "I bet you were at Kathy's house." Momma grabbed Lena by the back of her hair and said, "Does Kathy's house always wreak with cigarette smoke?" When Momma let go of Lena's hair, she shoved her against the door and said, "You won't be coming in here all times of the night after being out - doing who knows what with who knows who." "Do you think I'm crazy?" Lena adjusted her dress and slowly walked to her bedroom hurting and crying.

Lena didn't think about Tim until she had gotten a bath and laid down on her bed. She reached over to turn the lamp off and laid there in the dark, wondering where he was from, and why she had never seen him around town. About half an hour later, she fell asleep.

When Lena arrived at work the next day, she asked Kathy about Tim. Kathy replied, "You've never seen him because you never come out of the house or go anywhere." "Seriously though, he just got in town, and he's here to work at the new chemical plant near Highway 41." A week later, Kathy asked Lena to go with her to Bill's Place after work again, but Lena said she had laundry to do after work, and every night after that, she made up some excuse - not to have to deal with the wrath of her mother again.

# 4

## WAS IT WORTH IT?

Night after night, Lena would lay awake in her bed and think about Tim and how handsome he was. Even though she was short of words when she met him, Lena feared that he would take interest in somebody else if she didn't see him soon. For the first time in her life, someone was interested in her. A whole month had passed. It was Friday afternoon, and the weather was nice. Kathy begged Lena to come with her to Bill's Place, "Besides, Tim is still asking about you," she said. "Please, please…," Kathy begged, "If you don't come with me, I'll have to turn all the guys down by myself," she joked. "Girl you are so crazy," replied Lena. All Lena could think about was her mother waiting for her in the dark but then, she remembered, it's Friday night and her mother is playing Bingo. "Okay, I'll go, but just for a little while," she told

Kathy. They jumped in Kathy's car and they were off to Bill's Place. Kathy's favorite spot was occupied, so they took a seat at the bar. Before long, Lena felt someone touching her on the shoulder. She heard a whisper in her ear saying, "I've been waiting for you." When Lena turned around, it was Tim. There he stood, just as handsome as before, wearing a grey collared shirt, black slacks with a black leather belt, and shiny black leather shoes. The first two buttons of Tim's shirt were unbuttoned. Lena looked as if Prince Charming was there to return her glass slipper. He asked Lena if she would like to go outside and talk, she looked at Kathy, who was giving her the signal to go ahead. Tim and Lena went outside and talked for a little while. Lena found out that Tim was two years younger than her. That explains why he looked so young, but it didn't matter, she was still interested in getting to know him. Lena and Tim talked for about an hour, but it seemed like only five minutes had passed. Even though Lena knew Momma was playing Bingo, she had this feeling of dread and fear that she just couldn't shake. Lena knew it was getting late and she needed to get home before Momma, so she told Tim she enjoyed talking to him, and that she had better get back inside and find Kathy. "Well, can I at least get a hug?" asked Tim. Lena slowly reached up to give Tim a hug. In her mind, she thought, Tim's cologne smelled so good…too good to be in that bar with all that smoke. When they let go of each other, Lena looked down and Tim opened the door for her. When Lena stepped back inside Bill's Place, Kathy was surrounded by several guys, being the life of the party as usual. Lena and Tim could see that Kathy was surely not ready to go, so Tim volunteered to walk Lena home. At first, Lena refused, but then Kathy whispered in her ear, "The both of you can get to know each other better during your walk home." The more Lena refused to let Tim walk her home, the more he and Kathy insisted. Finally, Lena grabbed her apron out of Kathy's car and started walking down the sidewalk - in the direction of her apartment with Tim. During the walk, Tim told Lena about his family and where he was from. Lena told Tim about her two jobs, but she never mentioned anything about her family. When they got to the entrance of Lena's apartment complex, she turned to Tim and said, "Thanks for walking me home." Tim asked, "Are you sure you don't want me to walk you to the door, after all, what kind of gentleman would I be?" "No!' said Lena, abruptly, "I didn't mean to sound upset but this is fine. I'll talk to you later," and she rushed off towards her apartment. When Lena got inside the apartment, Momma was still at her Bingo game, so the foreboding feeling that she had in her stomach was for nothing.

Since Lena told Tim where she worked, he would go home after working at the chemical plant on Fridays to freshen up and meet her at the middle school in time to walk her home. Lena still wouldn't let Tim go any further than the entrance of the complex, out of fear that someone would tell her mother, especially Ms. Shirley, the candy lady who knew everybody's business in the complex.

Tim was falling for Lena and they enjoyed spending any amount of time together, even if it was just a walk home. Tim would pick goat grass with yellow blooms in the schoolyard, under the streetlight, and rope them together to make Lena a necklace while they walked to her apartment. One night, while walking Lena home, Tim asked, "Why don't you want me to meet your folks?" Lena's smile came to an instant halt. She paused, trying to think of the right words to say. "It's just not the right time." Tim reached into his pocket, and he pulled out a black velvet box and handed it to Lena. "What is this?" she said, "Just something I thought you would like." Lena smiled and said, "Thank you." She gave Tim a hug and a kiss at the entrance of the complex and held the box tightly while she made her way home. Lena was so happy! She couldn't stop smiling.

As soon as she stepped in the door and turned to close

it, Wham!!! Across the back with a leather belt, then again across the stomach. Momma's Bingo game had been canceled and rescheduled for another night during the upcoming week. Momma had spotted Lena and Tim's rendezvous under the streetlight from the window. Lena crouched down and tried to protect her face because Momma's belt seemed to be flying in all directions. Once before, she hit Lena in the face while in a heightened rage and Lena walked around with a welted bruise under her eye for a week. Liz heard what was going on, but she turned over in the bed and covered her ears with the pillow. "What did I tell you about hanging out all night, acting like a floozy?" "You think I don't know what's going on?" "So that's the guy you've been seeing, huh?" Lena squeezed the box that Tim gave her and ran to her room because Momma would not stop hitting her until she got out of sight. Lena placed the box under her pillow then she laid down on her bed and cried. A few minutes later, she got up, dried her tears, and ran her bathwater. As she sat in the tub, she was careful not to get soap on the red welts that ran up and down her arms, legs, and back. When Lena got out of the tub and went back to her room, she pulled the black box out from under her pillow and opened it. Lena let out a gasp and covered her mouth. It was a gold necklace with a charm that had a diamond in the center of a flower.

As Lena was holding the necklace in the air, Liz turned over in her bed that was on the other side of the room. "Where did you get that from?" she asked. "Well, I've been seeing this guy named Tim and he's very nice." Before Lena could finish, Aunt Liz sat up on the side of the bed. "That's beautiful Lena, but you can't wear that, Momma will see it," she whispered. "I know, but nobody has ever given me anything like this before," said Lena. When she finished admiring the necklace, she put it back into the box and placed it under her pillow. Lena pulled the string to turn the lamp off and they both laid down and went to sleep.

Lena had not gone to Bill's Place in weeks. When Tim showed up at the school the following Friday night, Lena sent Kathy outside to tell him that she would be driving her home, since they would be working late. Tim looked confused and he walked to the corner of the block and caught the bus back home. Lena needed time to figure things out as the tension between her and Momma was rising.

One night, Tim thought he would surprise Lena with his new car. Instead of walking, he would drive her home. Tim had purchased a sky-blue Lincoln Continental. He drove over to the middle school and waited for Lena to come outside. When he spotted Lena walking outside with Kathy, he got out of the car to meet her. Lena was startled, as Tim caught her off guard, but after talking to him, she agreed to let him take her home. When Lena got inside Tim's new car, she marveled at the interior. Tim didn't think to ask if she liked the gift that he had given her the other day, he just wanted to make sure their relationship was in good standing. Lena told Tim her feelings had not changed towards him, but she had been working longer hours. During the drive to Lena's apartment, Tim said, "I've been thinking," "Would you like to take our relationship to the next level?" Lena looked puzzled as she clenched her hands together. "What do you mean?" she asked. "We can get our own place, you know, and start our life together." Lena zoned out for a moment as she wondered, "What would her mother think and how would her sister and brother make ends meet without her? "Are you listening Lena?" asked Tim. "Yes, I'm listening," she replied, in an unsure tone. "We can move out into the suburbs, on the other side of town, and start our life together," Tim continued. "What do you think?" "I don't know what to say." "You mean you don't feel the same way about me as I feel about you?" "I didn't say that…it's just… she paused… let me think before we start making all these big decisions." "Alright, you think about it and I will meet you on Friday when you get off work." When Lena got home, she told Aunt Liz what Tim had said. Aunt Liz was quiet, she was happy for her, but she knew if Lena moved out, all their mother's anger would come down on her because Uncle Daniel was always at school or working. The financial responsibilities would be too much without Lena too. Aunt Liz imagined what that would be like for a moment, then she said hysterically, "You can't leave me here with Momma, I can't do this by myself, Daniel is never here, and I'll be the only one here having to contend with her!"

# 5

## A NEW LIFE

The next Friday, when Tim came to pick Lena up from work, she had no choice but to tell Tim about her family's financial predicament and why she couldn't leave. That evening, when Tim was dropping Lena off at her apartment, Uncle Daniel was going to play basketball with his friends, and he met Tim. They hit it off immediately, and Tim offered to help Uncle Daniel get a part-time job with him at the Chemical Plant. There were openings in the shipping and loading area. Uncle Daniel could start working full-time after graduating if he wanted. Working at the Chemical Plant would earn Uncle Daniel a lot more money, even if he only worked part-time, and it would be easier for him and Aunt Liz to take care of Momma and the bills.

Shortly afterward, Lena and Tim got married, nothing special, just a courthouse wedding. Lena wore her white Sunday dress, low heel pumps, and pearl earrings. Tim wore a black suit, white shirt, and black dress shoes. After the ceremony, they returned to Lena's apartment to gather the bags she had already packed. When Lena walked into her bedroom, Aunt Liz started crying and telling her how much she was going to miss her. Uncle Daniel walked into their bedroom and gave Lena a hug, congratulating and telling her how much he was going to miss her too. Uncle Daniel helped carry Lena's bags to Tim's car where she had asked him to wait. Momma didn't say a word as they passed by, she acted as if she was so hypnotized by what was on the television that she couldn't pull her eyes away. Lena didn't say anything either, she just glanced at Momma and kept moving. Lena had to go back inside the apartment to get the black box Tim had given her from under her pillow. When she went back to the door, Momma said, "You'll be back, it won't last long." "You don't sneak around behind your momma's back like that... and think everything is going to work out just fine." Lena started to feel guilty and somewhat cursed, instead of blessed by her mother's words. She pulled the door closed anyway. When Lena got to the bottom of the steps, she told Tim she was ready to go.

They found a starter home in the suburbs with a huge yard, just as Tim had promised. The house needed a lot of work, but they didn't care, they were happy, in love, and they had big plans for it. There were broken windows, a leak in the roof, the house needed painting on the inside and outside, and the porch was wobbly. With Tim's income, Lena could afford to stop working at the middle school at night. Lena and Tim had nice neighbors, the countryside was beautiful, and the house was looking better each day as they continued to work on it.

# 6

## THE ARRIVAL OF ME
## AND MY FRIENDS

A year after Tim and Lena were married, I was born. Three years later, my brother Ron was born and two years later my little sister Cindy was born. We attended Sunday service at Meadow Brook Baptist Church and my mother served on the Missionary Outreach Board. Ron and I sang in the Sunbeam Children's Choir. Aunt Liz and Uncle Daniel would come to visit and have dinner with us on Saturdays. Everything seemed to be looking up for our family.

Jake was the baby in his family, born to Roxie and James Jones. Hidden genes must have shown up in Jake because he was light-skinned with hazel eyes and he had curly brown hair, unlike his parents or siblings. Jake had an older sister named Charlotte and an older brother named Ralph.

Jake's mother was currently a homemaker but previously, she was a housekeeper in Glendale Estates, an upper-class white neighborhood. Roxie would also bring her employer's clothes home to launder, press, and make alterations to them. Even though Roxie had three children, you would not know it, she has one of those shapes that just bounce back after having a baby. Roxie has dark smooth skin and long black hair that she pins up in a bun while she does her daily chores. Her beauty often attracted the wrong kind of attention from her bosses, causing her to quit several house-cleaning jobs. Roxie would complain that the white women she worked for were mean, they did not want her touching anything expensive in their home, and they would watch to make sure she didn't steal anything either. The husbands, on the other hand, could not keep their eyes off her, for another reason. They watched every time she bent over to vacuum under a chair or sweep up the trash. When they said good-bye for the day and pat her on the shoulder, their hands always seemed to slip down her back, brushing her bottom. After Jake was born, Roxie stopped going to the white neighborhoods to clean houses altogether.

Jake's father is tall and slender, his complexion is slightly lighter than Roxie's. He works at the Steel Manufacturing Company on the first shift and he works at the bakery on the second shift. James's income provides his family with a decent home in the working-class community.

Our other friend - Matt was born to Marie and John Phillips. Both were natives of Alabama. Marie was very small in stature with curly black hair, John was very tall - as most of the men in his family were. Matt was a beautiful baby with a head full of curly black hair. It was prophesied that he had been touched by the hand of God and that he would become a preacher one day, operating in all gifts of the spirit. His mother was given instructions that no matter what, she had to bring him up in the church. Matt had a birthmark on his right arm - in the shape of angel wings. Marie always brought Matt to church, even though John preferred to stay home.

Matt's parents struggled during the first years of their marriage. John soon discovered marriage and family life wasn't for him. By the time Matt was six, he was very aware of how much his parents argued. When Matt was bored, he would often pull a chair from the kitchen table and bounce his favorite bouncy ball between his legs on the floor. Marie bought it for him out of the gumball machine at the grocery store. Matt would much rather be outside playing catch with his father, but John wasn't the athletic type and he seemed to only want to sit in front of the TV and have a beer when he was home from work.

One afternoon Matt was bouncing his ball in the kitchen. John came up the hall with a duffle bag filled with some of his clothes and a few other things. He squatted in front of Matt and told him that he was leaving because he and Marie just couldn't see eye to eye. Matt was six years old and did not know how to respond to his father's statement. Matt thought his father meant he was leaving for a little while to cool off and he would return the next day like always. Matt didn't say anything to his father, not knowing that would be the last conversation he would ever have with him.

# 7

# THE BEGINNING OF
# STRUGGLES

O ne spring afternoon, the sun was bright, and the breeze in the air carried the smell of honeysuckles. I was six, Ron was three, and Cindy was a year old. Ron and I were outside playing in the front yard, and Cindy was in the house taking a nap. Lena had the window up so she could hear her if she started crying while she was working in the garden. The phone rang. Lena got up, pulled her gardening gloves off, and started walking towards the house. When she answered the phone, it was Jane, the Secretary from my father's job. She said that he had an accident and had been checked into St. Peter's Hospital. His job was to lift buckets of chemicals and pour them into a larger machine. Jane explained that when my father picked up the bucket to pour the chemical mixture into the machine, he became dizzy, and fell to the floor. They knew he suffered chemical burns, but they did not know, to what extent or what else was going on with him.

Lena gathered me, Ron and Cindy, and asked Mrs. Parker, who lived next door if she would watch us while she went to the hospital to see about our father. Mrs. Parker was a retired high school teacher. She gave us milk and cookies and told us that everything would be alright. When Lena arrived at the hospital, our father was hooked up to a respirator. The nurse explained to Lena that he had suffered upper respiratory damage due to inhaling the chemicals over time, and he would most likely continue to need the respirator for a while. At that time, Lena didn't know how long my father would be out of work or if he would ever be able to work again. My father stayed in the hospital for another month before he was able to breathe without the respirator and was released to go home. By that time, the medical bills had started coming in the mail. Lena was already struggling to take care of us and the household expenses with her income alone. My father was very weak, he could not work at the chemical plant anymore or on the house. It would be several years before he was approved for long-term disability, so he started drinking. Lena would argue with him about having to take care of him and the children by herself. My father didn't finish high school either, so his limited education and work experience gave him few choices in the job pool. There was no way he could work while taking his medication anyway, since it made him nauseous and drowsy. By the time I was nine years old, my parents argued so much that my father decided - it would be best if he left, so he moved back home to live with his parents in Mississippi.

We made it through the summer and fall, but winter was brutal. Lena did the best that she could. The gas was turned off at the beginning of December and there was no firewood for the fireplace either. Me, my mother, Ron, and Cindy slept in the same bed to keep warm. There was a kerosene heater in the room that we shared, but it was about to run out of kerosene. A tree cracked under the pressure of the snow and hit the corner of the house, leaving a hole big enough to see the snow falling outside. Lena put a towel in the hole to help keep the cold out but there wasn't much she could do about the leak in the roof. We stayed there long as we could, but the mortgage notices kept coming. Lena finally accepted that my father wasn't coming back, and we had no other choice but to move in with my grandmother, Uncle Daniel, and Aunt Liz.

# 8

## MOVING DAY

It was an early Saturday morning, Uncle Daniel pulled in our driveway with a moving truck to help move some of our belongings to Meadow Creek Apartments and the rest went to storage. Once we had packed everything that we were going to take with us, we looked at our first home one last time, then we walked to the nearest bus stop to catch a ride to Meadow Creek Apartments. My father had taken the car with him when he moved back to Mississippi.

When we arrived at the apartment complex, there was a partial dirt field across the street, it looked like some boys were playing football. I was starting to miss having my own yard already. Lena turned around and told us to be on our best behavior when we get inside. She warned us that she had not seen her mother in a long time, and she did not know if she had changed or not. "What do you mean if she has changed or not?" I asked. "Well, she wasn't...kind...to me and my siblings." "Oh," I said. "Hopefully, we won't be here very long," said Lena. "Just long enough to get some money saved and back on my feet." Lena grabbed the stair rail to brace herself with Cindy in the other arm, and we proceeded to walk up the steps. Ron and I followed close behind. We were curious to see where our room would be in the apartment. Lena unlocked the door with her old key. When we got inside, she showed us where our room was. Uncle Daniel was putting the bunk bed together for me and Ron, in his room, on the opposite side of his bed. Lena and Cindy shared a bed in Aunt Liz's room.

When Uncle Daniel finished putting our beds together, I made up my bed with my blue sheets and brown flannel print quilt. When I finished, I went to Lena's room where she was changing her blouse, it had gotten dirty during the moving process. I asked Lena if the old lady sitting in the living room with the mean stare was her mother. "Yes, that's Momma." "What do we call her?" I asked. "Momma," Lena replied, "That's what all her children and grandchildren call her, even the ones that seldom visit." By that time, Momma busted in the door. "I told you, you'd be back… just a lot sooner than I thought!" Lena and I were both startled. "That's what happens when you sneak around doing stuff you don't have no business doing. I see you're not teaching these boys anything. Why is he in here with you while you're changing clothes anyway?" Momma looked at me and said, "Get out of here, and I better not catch you in here again while your momma is changing clothes!" I turned around slowly and walked back to my new room where Ron was. Lena didn't say a word. When I left, I could hear Momma saying to Lena, "So how long have you been undressing in front of those boys like that?" Lena always got dressed and undressed in the same room with us, she would take turns putting us in the bath with her when we were smaller, especially after my father became ill and left. I don't know if it was to save water or time since she was having to do everything by herself.

There was a floor model TV in the front room, but we couldn't watch it, so we found other things to do to keep ourselves busy. Lena wrote to let my father know that we had moved so that he would know where to find us if he decided to visit.

# 9

## THE RING

A few years had passed since my father had left, and we had not heard from him until one day, Lena went to the mailbox and there was a letter addressed from Mississippi. My grandmother wrote to tell us our father had passed.

We all loaded up in Uncle Daniel's car and he drove us to Mississippi. I was ten, Ron was seven, and Cindy was almost four. The drive was long and hot, with the windows down. The dirt road that my grandmother lived on seemed to go on forever. Finally, we arrived. We got out of the car in front of a big white house with lots of windows and a long porch with white rocking chairs. To the right of the house was my father's car, but it looked like it had not been driven in a long time. The tires were dry-rotted, and there were leaves embedded between the windshield and the hood. A light-skinned lady with white hair greeted us on the front porch, I assumed this was my father's mother. When we stepped onto the porch, she gave us a big hug and said, "It's so good to see ya'll, come in. How was the trip? Ya'll want something to eat? How about a cold glass of sweet tea?" My mother sat at the kitchen table holding Cindy because she was still asleep. Uncle Leonard, who lived with my grandmother, took me and Ron to the backyard to play on the tree swing and pick blackberries and honeysuckles.

After a while of getting caught up with everyone, we all got baths and something to eat. There was so much food, it seemed like everybody that came to the house brought food, sodas, or flowers. Lena decided that we should eat and figure out where we would sleep for the night. We didn't attend the wake that Friday evening, Lena thought it would be too much for us children to have to keep viewing the body. Lena slept on the sofa and Uncle Daniel slept on the recliner. Ron, Cindy, and I, slept on the floor on a stack of blankets.

We woke up Saturday morning and got ready for the funeral. The funeral home sent a car for us to ride to the church. Once we got there, I saw the hearse outside the church and lots of flower petals that had fallen off larger arrangements that had been carried inside the sanctuary. As our family lined up to march in and view the body one last time, I heard my Uncle Leonard telling Uncle John, who had flown in from Detroit that my father's drinking had gotten so bad that he would choose alcohol over his medication. Uncle Leonard continued... saying that one morning, at a time when my father should have been up watching the news, he was still asleep. My grandmother went to check on him and he wouldn't wake up.

When we got close to the casket, Lena just stared at my father. She didn't say a word or shed a tear. I remembered his face, but Ron and Cindy didn't. Then, Lena told me and Ron to come on, and we took our seats on the front row.

After the funeral service, my father was buried behind the little white church that my grandmother attended. We left the gravesite and went back to my grandmother's house. In the living room, Lena sat in the recliner while Me, Ron, and Cindy sat on the sofa. Uncle Leonard came in and sat beside me, he had an old photo album with pictures of my father. "Boy you sure do look like your father," he said. Lena glanced at the photos and looked away as if she was irritated by them, then she got up and went to the kitchen to get something to drink. When Lena returned, she told Uncle Leonard that I didn't just look like my father, but I had ways just like him too. I didn't know if she meant that - in a good way or a bad one.

We ate dinner at my grandmother's house, and everybody shared funny memories of my father. After a few hours had passed, Lena stood up slowly and said, "Well, it was good to see everybody again, but I guess it's time for us to be getting back home," "Well, I sure enjoyed ya'll...Don't let it be too long before ya'll come back to visit okay?" said grandma. As we got ready to load up in Uncle Daniel's car, Uncle Leonard said, "Hold on a minute." He squatted in front of me and put one hand on my shoulder while he reached inside his coat pocket with the other hand. "Here," he said. It was a silver ring with a black sapphire stone in it. "It was your father's. I figured it would mean more to you than me, and since you are the only one who is old enough to remember him, it would only be right for you to have it." "Thanks, Uncle Leonard," I said, "This is the only thing that I have that belonged to my father." I gave him a big hug and he said, "Ya'll take care," and he waved goodbye as we walked towards the car. I knew my father was gone forever unless I see him in heaven as the preacher said, but until now, I never had anything to remind me of him. This was the saddest, yet best weekend of my life. We had a long hot ride ahead of us. As we drove down the long dirt road, I put my father's ring on, and it was so big that it swung around my tiny finger.

When we got back home, Aunt Liz greeted us at the door and asked how the funeral was. Momma didn't ask about the funeral and we weren't expecting her to either. When I got inside my room, I placed the ring under my mattress, at the same time, Lena was passing by my room and she said, "Hand me that ring, I'll hold on to it so you don't lose it." It took all the strength I had - to walk over to the door and hand her the ring. The moment the ring left my hand and went into hers, I felt like I was losing my father all over again and I felt in my gut that I would never see that ring again. I turned and walked back to my bed slowly and I just laid there.

# 10

## WHICH WAS WORSE?

After we returned home, Lena's demeanor started changing, I don't know if it was good for her to see my father again, even in death. The funeral seemed to revive a lot of undesirable memories. She had false hope that one day he would recover and come back but the funeral confirmed that she would have to raise the three of us alone and it didn't help - to have to move in with Momma. After hearing all the stories about my father, I was starting to miss him, but Lena never had anything good to say about him, so I learned early on, to stop asking about him.

When times were better, Lena and I were very close. She would take me shopping with her. When she tried on dresses, I would zip the back or hold her purse and tell her how they looked on her. I think that's where I developed my eye for fashion. She showed me how to pick out towels, washcloths, and sheets, with the best quality of fabric by rubbing my fingers up and down the material and stretching them to see if they were durable. Now, Lena doesn't have much money to shop with, in fact, Ron and I are down to three pair of pants each, we wear them twice before we wash them. Lena doesn't talk to me that much anymore, and if she does, it's usually brief and hostile.

The next morning when I woke up to go to school, I felt the dread rushing back, remembering Lena had taken my father's ring from me, and if that wasn't bad enough, all of a sudden, I hear someone holler in a loud angry voice "Get up and get ready to go to school!" It was Momma, yelling at me and Ron. Lena had already left for work and dropped Cindy off at the babysitter. This was a big change. When we lived on the other side of town, the bus would come before Lena went to work. Now that we live closer to town, the bus picks us up much later - as it gets closer to the school.

We didn't have to change schools because we still live in the same district, but Lena had to find somebody else to keep Cindy during the day. Momma was home all day, but she would never keep Cindy, and Lena would be too afraid to leave Cindy with her. By the time Ron and I got dressed, brushed our teeth, and washed our face, Aunt Liz was already preparing grits, eggs, bacon, and coffee for Momma. I could hear Momma scolding Aunt Liz for cooking her eggs too hard. We were going to eat breakfast at school, so we grabbed our coats and went outside to catch up with the rest of the kids walking towards the bus stop at the entrance of the apartments. I met Jake and Matt on the first day that we went to school from our apartment. Their families lived outside the apartment complex but all the kids in the neighborhood seemed to travel together. I told them why we had moved to Meadow Creek Apartments, they were understanding about my situation. That day marked the beginning of our lifelong friendship.

Going to school wasn't bad, but after school, Jake and Matt would walk with me and Ron to the entrance of the apartments, then they would proceed to walk towards their homes. Ron and I had to choose which route we would take - to avoid the gangs that lingered throughout the divided sections of the apartments. We were too young to split up. One day, we decided to cut through a set of apartments and jump over a fence that separated the backyards. As soon as I lifted Ron over the fence and climbed over myself, there was a Rottweiler chained inside the back yard. I almost wet myself and Ron already had. We ran past the dog barking at us and cut between the apartments. We got back on the sidewalk and ran home.

When we got inside the apartment, Aunt Liz was still at Jolynn's. Uncle Daniel was at the Chemical Plant and Lena had picked up part-time work in the afternoons, braiding and fixing her clients hair throughout the apartments. Momma would be the only person who would be home with me and Ron after school. We tried to stay out of her sight, but it was impossible. She always had something for us to do. Momma would tell me to wash the dishes or mop the floor after she had her friends over while we were at school. Ron had to sweep the floors and dust the furniture. We had to lug our clothes and bed cover to the laundry-mat downstairs and across the street because Lena was too tired when she got home from work. When we returned from doing our laundry, we put everything away and made our beds. Momma made sure nothing was out of order on our side of the bedroom.

One afternoon, Momma was in the kitchen getting ready to bake a cream cheese pound cake. She called Ron to turn the TV to the news. He turned the knob on the floor model TV until it stopped on channel 2. Momma hollered for him to adjust the antennas on top of the TV so that the squiggly lines would go away. Ron tried but he couldn't get rid of the squiggly lines. "Come here," said Momma. Ron let go of the antennas slowly and started walking towards her... not knowing what was going to happen. Suddenly, I heard Ron crying, he came back in our room with flour all over his face and in his hair. "What happened?" I asked. "She hit me on the head with the flour sifter," he said. "Why do we have to stay here with her?" he cried. "Why can't we go back to our old house?" "I told you, Lena can't afford to take care of us by herself, and since daddy is never coming back, we have to stay here for a little while. Just try to stay out of her way." "I did," Ron retorted, "But she called me."

When Lena came home that night, we told her what had happened. She sat down on the bed and let out a deep breath, as if she was frustrated with us for bothering her with something that she could do nothing about. While Ron was going on and on, explaining what had happened to him and why we needed to leave, I could tell that Lena was becoming overwhelmed with life. The janitorial job at the hospital paid minimum wage, and she couldn't charge full price for doing hair because she didn't have a license. I'm sure, having to come home to Momma every day took its toll as well. The only thing that Lena would say to us was,

"Just stay out of her way, and when she says something mean and insulting to you, just sit there quietly and ignore her."

Lena got a bath and started cooking dinner. About an hour later, Aunt Liz walked in the door, she hung her apron in the closet and asked Lena what could she help her with. "I got it now, everything is cooking, I'm just waiting for it to get done," said Lena. Aunt Liz turned the pots down low and told Lena she needed to talk to her. They went into their bedroom and sat on the beds across from each other. "Lena, you have got to do something, Momma is beating those boys every day, whether they do anything wrong or not. Whatever demon she is harboring, she's taking it out on them. The other day, I came home early from work. I knew the boys should have been home by then. When I opened the closet door to hang up my apron, they were sitting in there. I didn't even ask why they were in there, I just told them to go to their room and be very quiet while I distracted Momma by asking her what she wanted for dinner. One day I came out of the bathroom because I heard her yelling at them, then everything got quiet. I stepped back into the bathroom to flush the toilet and I came out. I don't know what had happened, but she was punishing them by making them lie under her bed. I can't tell you how often I've seen her hit them with brooms or whatever she can get her hands on. Can you find something for them to do after school? If I try to stand up for them, she's likely to start pounding on me too." Lena already had a sitter for Cindy. Ron became friends with Tony, who lived downstairs when we first moved into the apartment. Lena asked Tony's parents if Ron could play with him after school sometimes and they said it would be all right. Ron started hanging out at Tony's apartment on the weekends too. I was the only one left with Momma every day.

One rainy Saturday afternoon, Momma was taking a nap on the sofa, or at least, I thought she was. Her head was tilted back, and she was snoring. I was watching Lassie on TV. During the commercial break, I got up and walked past her to get something to eat out of the pantry. She sat straight up, jerked me by the collar and said, "Don't you ever pass by me again without saying excuse me!" By the time she let go of me, I had lost my appetite. I went to my room with tears in my eyes and laid across my bed. I thought to myself… "If only my father was here, we wouldn't even be here".

Lena used to come home in between jobs to check on us, but lately, I think she works the second job to stay away from Momma and us. I guess she figured if she can't do anything about the situation, then why worry about it all the time. We don't bother to tell her about the things that Momma does to us anymore. She doesn't care anyway. I'm supposed to let somebody beat me and insult me every day, and I just take it. This whole thing about ignoring Momma, wasn't helping. Momma would get furious when I ignored her or acted as if it didn't bother me when she jerked or hit me. I was starting to develop an outer shell, as I was becoming immune to the abuse, but I kept ignoring her because I knew it made her angry. She would retaliate, but I knew she would eventually have to stop hitting me. Then, I would walk away.

Lena came home one night before I fell asleep. I couldn't believe she cared enough to come into my room and talk to me. She asked about school. I didn't say anything, I closed my eyes and turned over to face the wall. It felt good to ignore her too. She was changing and had been for a while. She acted as if she didn't want to be around us anymore, especially me. I couldn't understand why she had become so distant towards me. What did I do to her? She wasn't the one who had to stay with Momma every day. When daddy was alive and we lived at our other house, Lena would praise me all the time and call me her favorite little man in the whole wide world, especially when I looked after Ron or played with Cindy while she was busy. Those days have become distant memories.

# 11

## THE DAYS WE LIVED FOR

Meadow Brook Alabama was a small country town where everybody knew each other. It wasn't hard for us to hustle up money - to get our favorite snacks. Jake and Matt had jobs, delivering newspapers, and I mowed lawns and raked leaves. Ms. Shirley sold ice cream, chips, candy, and sodas to the kids in the neighborhood. Having a candy lady in our neighborhood was everything. Whenever I wanted a snack, I would go downstairs and across the street to the other side of the complex. The only exception to Ms. Shirley's, was the legendary Chocolate Ice-Cream Soda from Randall's Drugstore. I always went with Jake and Matt, a treat like that was too good to be enjoyed alone.

At Randall's Drugstore, Mrs. Linda worked behind the counter. She was a tall, slender, Caucasian woman with no curves and a slight hump in her back. I think she was somewhere in her late fifties. Her hair was strawberry blonde with pin curls that stood about four inches high and they never moved, just like a football helmet. Mrs. Linda wore vibrant red lipstick and rosy pink rouge on her cheeks. Whenever we opened the door to the drugstore, she would walk up to the counter wearing her pink apron and say, "What are you boys having today?" In a harmonic trickle, we would say, "Chocolate ice cream soda please." I think Mrs. Linda already knew what we wanted; she was just being polite. All three of us would stand there watching the soda come out of the dispenser and into the glass. Mrs. Linda would drop two large scoops of chocolate ice cream into the glass. The ice cream would sink halfway down the glass and fizz back up to the top. Each time, we gazed as if we had never seen it done before. Nobody makes chocolate ice cream soda like Mrs. Linda.

When it was warm outside, we usually sat on the bench in front of the drugstore, watching the cars pass by and indulging our chocolate ice cream sodas until the last drop. When we finished, we returned the glasses and started walking towards the field. Along with some other guys from the neighborhood, we lived for playing football on the undeveloped field - across the street from the apartments where I lived. Even though our football games were informal, Jake always felt the need to explain the rules, that's just the way he was. I didn't care, but Matt would say "Can we just play already?" We never took for granted any moment to be kids and not have to worry about the pressures of life.

After the game was over, we would walk with Jake to his house first. We could smell his mother cooking dinner all over the yard. Then I would walk with Matt to his house, then back to my apartment. Even though the football field was across the street from my apartment, walking Jake and Matt home, gave me a few more minutes away from Momma.

# 12

## SCHOOL

As far as school, Matt was very smart, and he took pride in his appearance too. Matt wore dress slacks, buttoned-up shirts, dress shoes and he carried a briefcase like he was going to work for Corporate America. Jake and I carried old back packs, we wore ragged jeans, old t-shirts, and dirty gym shoes. Clothes were the one thing Jake couldn't argue with Matt. On picture day, Jake showed up with a tie to wear with his t-shirt. Matt had to show him how to tie it. Otherwise, Jake probably would have tied it around his waist or made it into a wrist band. Matt's teachers deemed him the ideal student and his classmates looked up to him as well. His books were always accompanied by his little red New Testament Bible, just in case he needed to witness to a fellow peer. Matt prayed for everybody and everything. He blessed our food in the cafeteria, our snacks, he prayed for the people that honked in traffic while we were on the school bus, he even prayed for the souls of the road-kill that we passed on the way to school. One winter morning, I just knew he was going to resurrect a baby squirrel that had fallen out of a tree and froze on the sidewalk. Not only was Matt the peacemaker, but he avoided trouble at all costs which wasn't always easy to do in our neighborhood. It wasn't uncommon to prove your manhood, whether it was fighting, showing off your skills on the football field or on the basketball court. Matt even managed to disregard Jake's constant insults about Christianity.

I struggled in school, I often daydreamed in class and missed the entire lecture. Whenever I zoned back in, I was too afraid to ask the teacher to repeat anything I missed - for fear of being humiliated in front of the entire class. One day, the teacher called on me while I was staring out of the window at a blue robin perched on the window seal. I couldn't answer her question, so she moved my desk to the front of the classroom, and everybody started laughing at me. Whenever I had math homework, nobody at home could help me with it. When I stayed up late, waiting for Lena to get home, she would tell me that she struggled in math when she was in school and she couldn't help me either.

One day, I came home with a bad report card. I got a beating by Momma and Lena. "You're not going to flunk out of school and become an alcoholic like your father," she would yell. At that moment, Lena confirmed, when she looked at me, she saw my father, and the older I became, the more pronounced his features were in my appearance and demeanor.

I think Jake's teachers dreaded to see him coming and couldn't wait to see him going. He had to question every part of the lecture, no matter what class it was. Jake was a "Know It All." He had these old fashion views about everything, and he didn't like having female teachers. He thought women had their place in society, but teaching a man certainly wasn't one of them. Despite all of that, Jake was very athletic, and he made pretty good grades.

One day, we were entering Meadow Brook Middle School, Principal Larkin was standing at the door greeting all the students. She pulled me aside for some reason and asked how was I doing? "Fine," I responded, "Are you sure?" "Yes, mam." I started walking away slowly towards the cafeteria to catch up with Jake and Matt to get my breakfast. I could feel Mrs. Larkin's eyes still peering over her glasses at me. She wasn't intimidating, but she made me feel a little uncomfortable that day.

One thing that I did look forward to at school was Science, and one Friday, we dissected frogs in Mrs. Well's class. I made sure to be there on time. When I arrived at the classroom, Mrs. Wells was standing outside the door, as usual, waiting to greet everyone. Her perfume always smelled good, her hair was pressed, and she wore long dresses with floral print that swayed back and forth as she walked. As I passed by her, I noticed that Lewis Hayes was already in his desk - looking sneaky as usual, he was known for his bullying and pranks. After everyone entered the classroom, Mrs. Wells closed the door and walked toward her desk, explaining what we would be doing. She reached for her grade book to call roll and assign us to the groups that we would be working in.

Mrs. Wells stepped to the left to sit in her chair. Before she could open the desk drawer to pull out the safety goggles, she realized she was sitting on something cold and wet. Mrs. Wells jumped up and turned around to see what it was. It was a frog from the lab. She yelled, "Who did this?" "No one is moving until I find out who did it!" Lewis and Carl pointed at me. I had learned that defending myself just got me into more trouble at home, it was considered talking back. I figured Mrs. Wells wouldn't believe me anyway. I couldn't muster up enough courage to stand up for myself, so I just sat there with an angry look on my face. "Is that true Timothy?" "Did you put the frog in my chair? Timothy, this doesn't seem like your behavior, but if you don't tell me anything different, I am going to have to send you to the Principal's office." She handed me a hall pass and told me to go to Mrs. Larkin's office. "You will receive a zero for this lab assignment," she said.

I gathered my belongings, zipped my backpack, and walked over to open the door. When I stepped outside the room and closed the door behind me, Lewis was grinning and pointing his thumbs back at himself, mouthing the words, "I did it." If I told on him, he would probably beat me up in the restroom or the locker room. When I got to the office, I sat on the chair and didn't say anything. The school Secretary called Principle Larkin from her office to come out and speak to me. "Timothy, I'm surprised to see you again," she said. When she asked why I was in the office, I still didn't say anything. She went back to her desk and pulled my schedule, then she paged Mrs. Wells and asked her what had happened. Principal Larkin threatened to call my mother and she did. I knew I was going to get into trouble if Lena had to leave her job at the hospital to come up to my school. Lena came to the office and Principle Larkin told her what Mrs. Wells had said. When Lena questioned me about it, I was silent, not even a budge. I was suspended from school for 3 days. When Lena got home, she came in my room and yelled at me, I gazed at the floor and zoned her out.

# 13

## I WISH IT WAS JUST A DREAM

Despite Lena's absenteeism in our lives, Ron managed to become her favorite child, not even Cindy could compare to him. Lena never yelled at Ron. He had her wrapped around his finger. She always brought something home for him, even if it was just the rest of her lunch. When I would ask Ron, what did she bring him, she would look at me and say, "Go on, you know you're too old to be taking things from your little brother."

Ron wanted to play football, but he needed to lose twenty pounds to make the team. Lena took him to a dietician. He was given a diet and exercise plan. He did neither and he didn't lose any weight. I could afford to slim down a little, since I had been frequenting Ms. Shirley's, so

I disciplined myself to run every day after school and I would skip lunch. I lost a significant amount of weight in a few weeks, but Lena never noticed.

Uncle Daniel was making good money at the Chemical Plant, now that he was working full time, so he paid most of the rent, allowing Lena to save more than she was able to in the past. She was afraid to purchase another house and try to take care of the three of us alone. Lena stopped fixing hair for extra money when she left the hospital in the afternoons and she started hanging out with Kathy again. One night, I was having a hard time falling asleep and I couldn't stop tossing and turning. Ron was already asleep, and Uncle Daniel had not come home yet. I heard someone come in the front door. Then I heard my grandmother yelling, but no one responded to her accusations. My grandmother was saying. "I'm not watching those kids while you're out in the streets all night with this man and that man." I got out of my bed slowly, as the apartment had creaking floors. When I got to the door, I peeked through the crack to see whom my grandmother was yelling at. Once I was able to focus my eyes on her, she raised her hand and struck my mother to the floor. She continued to yell, "If you wouldn't have had those children with that sorry excuse for a man, ya'll wouldn't be staying here." I dived back into the bed and covered my head.

The next morning, I jolted awake, but it was still dark outside. I was hoping what I had witnessed the night before was just a bad dream. It wasn't long before the recollections flooded my memory clearly. Daylight was fast approaching, and no one had come to wake me and Ron for school. I got off my bed and looked up at Ron on the top bunk, he was such a hard sleeper, still snoring and drooling on his pillow. I shook him once, then again real hard. Rubbing his eyes, he said, "What is it, Timothy?" "Wake up, it's time to go to school and Momma didn't come and wake us up." "Hurry up before the bus leaves us." Every morning, we walked with all the other kids that lived in our apartment building. By that time, my grandmother was already yelling at us, Aunt Liz was preparing coffee and breakfast for her. "Don't over-cook my eggs either," Momma yelled while watching the morning news. Ron wanted some of what Aunt Liz was cooking, but I told him to come on, he could eat breakfast at school. I helped him put on his coat and book-bag. We ran towards the door, then we heard Momma yell, "COME BACK HERE!" We turned and went back. "Don't you run in this house again!" "Now walk to the door like you got some sense!" We walked slowly to the door, carefully closing it behind us, and walking down the steps. When we got to the end of the sidewalk, Jake and Matt were waiting. "Man, what took you so long?" said Jake. "Our grandmother forgot to wake us up." Matt had his red testament in his hand.

When we got to school, we sat in the cafeteria, Matt blessed everybody's food and we ate. Jake would always tell Matt he didn't have to bless his food, if he should get poisoned and die, it must be his time to go. Jake would go on to say that he would be returning to the dirt with the worms and insects, instead of floating off into the sky to join some heavenly host.

# 14

## NEW BEGINNINGS
## FOR MATT

Matt was 12 when his mother remarried. Marie had two more children with her new husband Lou, who was a truck driver. Matt had a hard time forming a relationship with his stepfather. After all, if his biological father left, how did he know that Lou would stick around. Matt cut the grass and did a lot of chores around the house to help his mother. With two new siblings, there wasn't much time for Marie to spend with Matt. Whenever dinner was served, Matt would always bless the food. Marie would bow her head and smile as she could see the prophecy over his life coming to fruition every day. It was often quiet at the dinner table as Lou never had much to say and Marie had to encourage a conversation. "How was your day Lou?" "Same as every day," he replied. Matt could see that Lou's enthusiasm towards family life was starting to dwindle, especially since the family had grown so fast.

One day, Matt came home from school and set his briefcase against the wall. He heard a sniffle and a sigh coming from the kitchen. Matt walked slowly in the direction of the sound and there he found his mother sitting at the kitchen table. Marie looked up, drying her eyes and she said, "Hey Matt, how was school?" Matt knew Marie was covering up something, he was wise beyond his years. "School was fine mom but what's wrong?" After taking a deep breath, she said, "I have to go back to work, so I need you to be the little man that you are so good at and help watch Spencer and Laura." Matt already felt as though he was the man of the house. "Sure momma," he said, rubbing Marie on the back and giving her a hug. "But what happened? Why are you going back to work?" Well, she paused, "Lou won't be back," as if she didn't see it coming. Matt was not surprised that Lou had left, in fact, he knew why. He was reminded of what he had seen the other day.

Monday afternoon Marie had sent Matt to the grocery store to get some milk and eggs. On the way home, the bag started getting heavy. Matt decided to cut through the cemetery, a shortcut that most people took when traveling to and from town on foot. The path led to the railroad tracks and the place where Matt stepped off the tracks was near Ms. Joanne's house. The curtains in her living room were open. Matt saw her and Lou on the sofa with their arms around each other. Matt was angry, but not enough to tell Marie because he didn't like to see his mother hurting. At that moment, Matt thought to himself, this all makes sense. That's why Ms. Joanne was smiling at Lou at the gas station a few weeks ago. Lou was pumping gas, and Ms. Joanne was at another pump. When she walked towards the store to pay for her gas, she smiled at Lou and he couldn't keep his eyes off her. Marie never looked up, she was busy telling Spencer and Laura to sit still in the back seat. Lou got back into the station wagon after pumping the gas and drove out of the parking lot as if nothing had ever happened.

Marie's failed relationships were starting to take a toll on Matt's self-esteem. He had become self-conscious when they went to the grocery store as women would stare and whisper. He assumed they were talking about his mother, whether they were or not. Even worse, the ladies at church started pretending they forgot to invite her to events. Marie seemed to overlook a lot of things, but Matt was very observant, and nothing got passed him.

Marie had started working at the bakery and Matt took on the role of being the "Little Man" around the house, just like his mother needed him to. He would watch his little brother and sister after school and fix them something to eat while Marie was working late. Things were going well enough for Marie to enroll in Culinary School. She was an excellent cook and wanted to start her own catering business.

Matt had become very comfortable with the family dynamics. Things were back to normal and he liked having a routine each day. Matt was gifted in his ability to comprehend scriptures and ancient texts. When he wasn't helping around the house, he was studying his bible. He was the youngest person in the church to teach Sunday school. Matt and Marie had deep discussions about the bible during dinner. Matt encouraged Marie and she praised him. Marie appeared to be content with the way things were going as well.

# 15

## AN UNEXPECTED SURPRISE FOR THE JONES FAMILY

James would always leave for work before sunrise and Roxie would walk with Jake to the bus stop to meet his friends. By the time she got back, Leon would be getting ready to leave for work. Roxie may not have approved of the flirty gestures from her previous employers, but that didn't mean she shunned all flirtatious advances. Leon lived across the street. He had his own landscaping business. Leon wasn't much to look at, he was slim, poorly groomed, his hands felt like sweaty gravel, but he was quite the lady charmer. Whenever the opportunity presented itself, Leon would say, "Good morning Mrs. Roxie, how are you doing today?" Roxie always responded, "Fine Leon, and yourself?" Leon would usually say something like, "I'm fine Mrs. Roxie but I would be doing much better if I were over on that side of the street." "Boy, you are so crazy," Roxie would reply, and make her way back into the house. Sometimes, Roxie would notice Leon's wife, Virginia peering at her through the window and snatching the curtains closed.

Roxie didn't have many friends in the neighborhood, she sold moonshine, which kept a lot of married men at her house, especially while her husband was working. Beside the front door, was a small wooden table with a drawer. Inside the drawer, Roxie kept a tab book with the names and debts owed by all her customers. Roxie had a beautiful vegetable garden behind the house, where she hid the moonshine in baby food jars. When somebody wanted to make a purchase, she would go outback and pull a jar out of the soil, bring it inside to wash the dirt off in the sink, and towel dry it before giving it to the customer. Several city officials were regular customers, and because of that, Roxie never knew when she might be ratted out.

One mid-day afternoon, Roxie was home alone preparing dinner and she heard a knock at the front door. "Just a minute," she yelled from the kitchen. When she got to the front door to open it, the Sheriff was standing there. Roxie could hear her heart beating between her ears. She opened the door and said, "How can I help you?" "Do you mind if I take a look around?" He asked. "What for?" Roxie asked. "A neighbor reported a fluctuation of unfamiliar vehicles coming into this neighborhood but mostly stopping at this house." "Is that right?" replied Roxie. "Well, I launder and press clothes on the weekends, so it could be some of my clients, but you can look around if you want to." While the Sherriff looked around the living room, Roxie took that opportunity to go back into the kitchen. There was a jug of moonshine on the counter-top, she had nowhere to stash it, but she knew she had to play it cool. Roxie plugged the sink, poured dish detergent in it, and turned the faucet on. By the time the Sherriff got to the kitchen, the bubbles had filled the sink. Roxie held the jug of moonshine under the water and she appeared to be very calm. The Sherriff assumed she was washing dishes.

"Do you mind if I take a look out back?" "Go right ahead," she said. The moonshine equipment was well tucked away, about a mile into the woods. The Sheriff looked around then he came back inside, letting the screen door slam shut behind him. "Nice garden you got out there, I guess I'll be going now. I'll let myself out," and he walked back to the living room. Roxie was still half-way turned to the sink, moving the other hand under the water as if she was hunting silverware. "You have a nice day

Sheriff," she replied. Roxie never took her hand out of the soapy water until she heard the Sherriff's car pull out of the yard and drive up the road. She let the water out of the sink, put the moon shine on the counter-top and got a towel to dry her hands and the jug. When she went to the front window of the house to see if anyone saw the Sheriff leave her house, she glanced across the street and there was Virginia, Leon's wife peering right back at her, then she closed her curtains abruptly. Roxie knew this wasn't good. When James got home that night, she told him about the Sheriff's visit. A few months later, they decided to let the moonshining business phase-out and Roxie applied for a part-time job at a sewing factory.

Even though the moonshine business had come to an end, it didn't keep the guys from flirting with Roxie. One afternoon, Roxie was walking to the mailbox, and Charlie drove by, He was light-skinned with freckles and he had hazel-green eyes. When he saw Roxie, he couldn't help but to stop and say something. With his arm hanging out of the window, Charlie said, "You got the prettiest dimples I've ever seen Mrs. Roxie," she just smiled and admired the compliment, until she noticed Virginia across the street, getting out of her rocking chair to go back inside the house and slamming the screen door behind her. "It was good to see you Charlie, but I better get back to what I was doing now," said Roxie. Charlie put his arm back in his truck window and waved good-bye. As he smiled and drove away, he watched Roxie in his rear-view mirror until she was out of sight.

The Jones family didn't attend church. When James was younger, his mother took him to Meadow Brook Baptist Church, but his father despised all preachers. Every night, James would say grace at dinner, and he talked to his children about living right whenever he got a chance. Since James wasn't around that much, his father had the biggest influence on Jake. Jake visited his grandfather a lot when he was young. He gave Jake a lot of advice, I wouldn't say it was all good though. Jakes's grandfather told him what kind of cars to buy, what kind of women he should date, and how to save his money. Jake's grandfather was mean to his wife, but she tolerated him. Even though he was married, he told Jake to never fall in love with a woman. "The day you give your heart to a woman is the day she'll break it and run off with someone else," he would say. He told Jake to never let a woman know how much money he had either. Jake's grandfather never missed an opportunity to tell him how crooked preachers were and how they took the church offerings to pay for their expensive cars and how they dated all the women in the church - even the married ones. Jake believed everything his grandfather told him.

Ralph was seven years older than Jake and he could talk his parents out of anything, especially his mother. By the time Ralph was sixteen years old, he had convinced his parents to buy him a car. He had a yellow 67'Camaro. Ralph spent most of his afternoons at the skating rink, he wasn't much of a skater but all the girls in the neighborhood thought he was so cute.

Charlotte was four years older than Jake, she was beautiful, just like her mother. She had dark brown skin, dark brown eyes, and long black hair. Unlike Jake, Roxie always made sure Charlotte had the finest of everything. She was always dressed pretty, her outfits had matching shoes, trinkets, earrings, and necklaces.

# 16

## THE VISIT

Several years ago, on a Saturday morning, we were all at Jake's house, building a fort outside with broken tree limbs. We were in the 4th grade, Charlotte was in the 8th, and Ralph was in the 11th. A white Toyota Celica pulled in the driveway and we all stopped and stared. We were trying to figure out who was in the car that we had never seen before. When the driver turned the engine off, Jake ran inside the house to tell his father that a strange car was outside. James was lying on the sofa, after all, it was Saturday and he was relaxing while Roxie was in the laundry room ironing clothes. Before James could make it to the door, there was already a knock. As James slowly opened the door, squinting at the bright sunlight, there stood a petite light-skinned woman with a teenage boy who looked to be about Ralph's age. Jake was standing there still trying to figure out who these strange people were on their front porch. "Go play Jake," said James. "Tonya," said James, sounding confused. "What are you doing here?" Jake was peaking from beside the house, still trying to figure out who this woman was and how did his father know her?" Tonya replied, "This is Jacob and he's your son, James. There was no denying that Jacob looked more like James than his children with Roxie. James had so many thoughts bombarding his head at that moment. He thought to himself, "Why did she wait so long to tell me and how am I going to tell Roxie and the children?" A few minutes later Roxie had come out of the laundry room and made her way to the door, as she could see her husband and two other silhouettes through the sheer curtain. When Roxie opened the door, she was shocked to see Tonya standing on her front porch. Roxie knew all too well who Tonya was, she was dating James when Roxie met him, but James fell head over heels for Roxie. James turned to Roxie and said, "Roxie you know Tonya," and Roxie replied, "Yes but what is she doing here?" "Well, Tonya said this young man is my son." "Oh, is that right," asked Roxie, tilting her head back as the words slowly rolled out of her mouth. Roxie had a blank stare at first then she turned and went back inside the house. James knew Roxie was upset as his eyes followed her back inside the house then he turned back to Tonya slowly and looked down at the porch for a few seconds. Roxie was too calm for such surprising news. She had her flirty ways with the guys, but she was very jealous of James.

James stayed on the porch, as he had a lot of questions for Tonya. After a few minutes, Tonya and Jacob got back into the car and backed out of the driveway. The Celica went up the road and out of sight but that would not be the last time the Jones's would see them. When James returned inside the house, Roxie was quiet. James sat down beside her on the navy green sofa, moving the pillows aside so that he could sit closer to her. He grabbed Roxie by the hand, but she just sat there quiet and angry. "I didn't know Roxie, but now that I do, I told them it would be okay if Jacob started visiting." All Roxie could think about was James and Tonya building a new relationship around their son. Roxie snatched her hand away from James, leaving him sitting on the sofa alone. Roxie despised Tonya and the thought of her having a child by her husband and showing up every week was unbearable. She never imagined the wrath of taking James from Tonya would come back to haunt her like this.

That night everybody came in to wash up for dinner. Roxie had prepared pot roast, mashed potatoes, green beans, and cornbread. Charlotte and Ralph had been at the skating rink, so they missed everything. "Why is everybody so quiet?" asked Ralph. "Who was the lady and boy that came to the house earlier?" asked Jake. Roxie got up from the table and went down the hall to her bedroom with tears in her eyes. "What lady and boy?" asked Charlotte. James got up from the table and followed Roxie. Nothing had ever come between them before now.

That night, Jake heard his parents argue like never before. Roxie yelled, "What do you mean you didn't know?" "If you think Tonya is going to start showing up at my house every week, you are certainly mistaken." "Listen to me Roxie," pleaded James, "That's my son. I didn't know just like you didn't know. She was pregnant at the time we split up and she said she was so angry with me that she didn't want Jacob to have anything to do with me. She said the boy kept asking about me and she knew she had to tell him the truth one day."

As the days went by, Roxie's demeanor changed, she became bitter towards James and friendlier towards the men in the neighborhood.

Saturday morning Roxie had gone to the grocery store because she was out of flour, she was going to bake a lemon pound cake. When Roxie returned home, she saw

Tonya's car parked in the yard. James had his head in the window on the driver's side where Tonya was. Roxie didn't know what they were talking about but James sure was happy. When he saw Roxie, he brought the conversation and laughter to a halt. He stepped away from the car, waving and saying, "I'll see ya'll later." Roxie walked inside the house, not even acknowledging Tonya and slammed the door. Tonya backed out of the driveway and drove up the road still laughing. When James walked inside the house, Roxie said, "I thought I told you I didn't want to see her in my yard again." "Besides, what was going on when I pulled into the driveway, you and Tonya catching up on lost times?" James was silent for a moment then he said, "We were talking about how much Jacob and I have in common?" "Really? After all these years? How do you even know that's your child?" Roxie was very angry, but she knew in her heart that Jacob looked a lot like James when she got a little glimpse of him the first day he and Tonya showed up at the house." James disregarded Roxie's statement and said, "I just want to spend time with my son Roxie, that's all." Roxie just couldn't shake the idea of having another woman at her house every week and besides, what was that nosey Virginia thinking, across the street? Roxie continued to ignore James while measuring the ingredients for the cake. "Well fine Roxie, I don't know what else to say," said James.

James's parents lived on the same plot of land back up on the hill behind them. When Tonya would bring Jacob to visit, James would take him to his parent's house and that's where they would stay until Tonya came back to pick him up. One day Roxie was in the kitchen washing dishes and she looked out the window and saw James and Jacob walking to James's parent's house. Jake got up from the table handing Roxie his cereal bowl, then he asked, "Momma, who is that boy that daddy is always walking with to grandma and grandpa's house?" Ralph walked in the kitchen and said, "Yeah Momma. Is it true? Is he really daddy's son? Is he our brother?" Clearly, Roxie could see there was no denying that Jacob was James's son each time she saw him, but she replied, "Who knows, that could be anybody's child." "Tonya had quite the reputation." Roxie's bitterness continued to grow, James slept on the sofa, and their relationship grew further apart as they failed to communicate.

# 17

## A DOOR LEFT OPEN

Monday morning, after James had left for work and the children were getting ready for school, Roxie told Ralph to go down the street to give Charlie a package. "Just run it down the street and don't get in that loud car of yours," she said. "What is it anyway?" "I'm going to be late for school," said Ralph. Just do what I said, scolded Roxie. She knew Ralph liked to rev up his engine and she was afraid that it would draw too much attention if someone saw him dropping a package off at Charlie's house that early in the morning. Ralph thought his mother had wrapped Charlie a piece of the lemon pound cake and she wanted to catch him before he left for work. Little did Ralph know, it was a sponge with a note on it, wrapped in aluminum foil, inside a paper bag. The note informed Charlie that James had left for work and to come over around 8 o'clock. That would give Roxie time to walk Jake to the bus stop to meet me and Matt. Ralph returned home, and he and Charlotte left for school. The plan worked, shortly after everyone had left, Charlie came walking through the path and knocked on the back door. Roxie came to the door and there stood Charlie smiling with open arms, they didn't even make it to the bedroom.

Roxie periodically sent Ralph to drop off packages at Charlie's until one morning he refused to do so. "I know what's going on!" yelled Ralph, "And I won't be a part of it anymore, you better hope daddy doesn't find out! Really mom? Charlie? You fool around with Charlie? Isn't he supposed to be daddy's friend? You think I don't know what's going on?" Roxie flew into a rage. "Get out! Just get out!" she shouted. "You'll probably be just like James too, that's the only reason you wanted that car. Every night you're at that game room or the skating rink with this girl and that one." Ralph slammed the door and left for school. He knew his father was a good man and there was nothing he could do about Jacob.

One Saturday afternoon Roxie was in the house helping Charlotte pick out a dress and some shoes to go to her friend Judy's birthday party. James had just come home from work. As he was getting the mail, he saw Charlie coming down the road. James threw up his hand, but Charlie kept going like he didn't even see him. James knew he had been working a lot and hadn't had time to hang out with Charlie in a while but that was still no reason for him not to speak. "Maybe he had something on his mind," James thought to himself. While James was closing the mailbox, he heard a high-pitched voice calling his name. The sound was coming from across the street, so he turned to see who it was. It was Virginia sitting on her front porch. James threw up his hand to wave at her then he turned back around. James wasn't very fond of Virginia, she had never been a friendly neighbor, and she was always in everybody's business. Virginia sat her glass of tea on the table beside her rocking chair. She grabbed the bottom of her long black skirt to keep it from dragging along the ground as she made her way across the street to where James was. "How have you been James?" she asked. "I've been good Virginia and how have you been?" he replied. James just knew Virginia was eventually going to ask him about the lady and boy that had been visiting his house. "Isn't it funny how we think we know people, but we really don't?" said Virginia. Here we go, thought James. "Sometimes we don't even know what's going on right around us, even under our own roof," she continued. James was silent, standing there looking confused. Virginia paused and looked at him to make sure he was internalizing her parable, then she said, "Well, it was good to see you James. I have to go and check on my peach cobbler in the oven." "Take care," and she raised the bottom of her skirt and walked back across the street, stopping to pick up her glass of tea before she went inside the house. James closed the mailbox and walked inside the house, trying to figure out what that was all about. By that time, Roxie was coming out of the front door, she was walking Charlotte to Judy's house. Virginia had taken the cobbler out of the oven and returned to the front porch with her glass of tea. When Roxie looked across the street, Virginia smiled and waved at her with slight wiggly fingers. Roxie didn't know what Virginia meant by that gesture, so she turned her head the other way and kept walking Charlotte towards Judy's house. Charlotte could have gone to the party herself, but Roxie had one friend that she knew would probably be there.

Upon arriving, they followed the sound of the music around the house to the garage. When Charlotte arrived at the birthday party and took her sweater off, you would have thought it was her birthday. She was so beautiful with her pink dress, matching pearl earrings and necklace, pink shoes, and her hair had baby doll curls. Charlotte walked over to Judy and said, "Happy Birthday," and she gave her the gift she had brought her. Roxie stood at the entrance and scanned the room to see if she could spot Helen. There was no sign of her, but Roxie did notice all the other women staring at her and whispering, even Judy's mother. Judy was so excited to see Charlotte, she thanked her for the gift and told her to come inside to her bedroom. She wanted Charlotte to see the diamond bracelet that her father had given her. When Virginia's daughter Candace, showed up, Judy's mother sent her inside to Judy's room. Candace found Judy and said, "Happy Birthday, your mother told me I could sit your gift on the table in the garage." Candace noticed Charlotte standing there, and she looked at her, as if she was contagious. Charlotte didn't know why Candace was staring at her like that. Just when Judy was about to say, "We can go back to the garage now," Candace looked at Charlotte and said, "My momma said your momma likes Mr. Charlie who lives down the street." "What?" said Charlotte, looking confused. "My momma told Mrs. Lucile that Mr. Charlie comes to see your momma when your daddy goes to work." "That's not true!" "Yes, it is." "My momma wouldn't lie," said Candace. Judy didn't say anything but her facial expression revealed that she had heard the rumor too. Charlotte ran out of Judy's room to find Roxie and tell her that she wanted to go home. Roxie didn't know what had happened to Charlotte, she had been talking about going to Judy's party for a month. "Don't you want to stay at the party?" "No," she cried, "I just want to go home." "But you spent so much time getting ready, are sure you don't want to stay?" "No, let's just go, momma." Roxie looked at Judy's mother. Everybody was silent. "We're just going to go home, thanks for inviting us, I hope Judy enjoys her birthday," said Roxie. While they were walking home, Roxie asked Charlotte what happened. "Candace is always talking about people. She said you liked Mr. Charlie." Roxie couldn't swallow... neither could she find the words to make Charlotte feel better. Roxie felt it would be best if she just held Charlotte's hand and not say another word all the way home.

Roxie decided to stop seeing Charlie, but she wanted to tell him in person. Monday morning James left out early for work, but he returned about thirty minutes later. He told Roxie he forgot his timecard and couldn't clock into work without it. Roxie didn't say a word, she just kept getting dinner ready since she didn't have to be at work for a couple of hours. Wednesday morning, Roxie heard a knock on the back door, it was Charlie and she knew it was him before she opened the door. Her heart began to pound. She didn't know if she should open the door or not. Charlie kept knocking harder and harder until she finally opened the door. The first thing that came out of Roxie's mouth was, "Charlie this has to stop, we can't see each other anymore, the neighbors are talking, and I think James might be on to us too. He pretended like he left his timecard at home this morning, which he never does. He always leaves it in his car when he gets off work, so he doesn't forget it in the house. He needed an excuse to come home and see if I was up to something." Charlie acted as if he didn't hear a word she said. He charmed Roxie into letting him stay that day and he continued to come back. Charlie was showing up regularly on the days that Roxie wasn't scheduled to go to work. He had become so comfortable with their routine that he didn't even bother to travel the path anymore. One day Charlie came walking up the street, the coast seemed clear, so he darted across the ditch into Roxie's yard and walked up towards the front porch. He knew the front door would be unlocked after the children went to school, so he let himself in. Roxie was in the bathroom straightening up. Suddenly, she felt someone grab her from behind, breathing on her neck and the two of them went to her bedroom. Charlie pulled the front door behind him, but he didn't bother to make sure it was closed. Roxie nor Charlie would be prepared for what would happen next. James pretended to leave for work, but he had parked his car at the top of the road and walked down the street to their house. When James got to the front porch, he noticed the door was slightly opened. At first, he thought maybe one of the children had forgotten to close it on the way out to school but then his suspicion got the best of him. James walked in and pulled the door up behind him, leaving it slightly opened so that he didn't make a sound, then he walked slowly down the hall to the bedroom. It was what he suspected all along, his best friend and Roxie. Charlie caught sight of James first, but he was speechless and so was Roxie, once she figured out what Charlie was gazing at.

"I knew it all along, I just didn't want to believe it!" Roxie knew she had messed up now. Ironically, all she could think about was how important her family was to her and keeping it together. For the first time, she was able to see Charlie as a wimp and a coward as he pleaded with James and apologized. Then a flood of worries and uncertainties overwhelmed Roxie. What have I done? I let this man come into my home and destroy everything I have, she thought. Suddenly, she realized how important James was and now the child he had with Tonya wasn't as bad as he seemed to be all this time.

Unfortunately, James would be leaving for good and

never coming back. As he packed his belongings, he mumbled to himself, "All she had to do was keep the house and raise the children, she really didn't even have to work but no…, I work two jobs every day and before I can get up the road she's got my best friend in my house." When James reached the door, he looked back at Roxie and said, "You tell the kids why I left!" Roxie went back to the bedroom and slammed the door. She had always been very stubborn.

That evening when the kids got home from school, Roxie didn't say anything. They ate dinner without James, which was not unusual because James worked late sometimes at his second job, but he always came home afterward, no matter how late it was.

Roxie knew James was upset but she still had not internalized the ramifications of her actions. She could only see the situation from her point of view. It was Saturday morning, Roxie cooked buttermilk biscuits, sausage links, fried green tomatoes, grits, and red devil eye gravy. In the back of her mind, she thought perhaps James would find it in his heart to forgive her, or he would miss the children and come walking in the door. She would have his favorite breakfast prepared. After all, James loved Roxie's cooking. Roxie listened expectantly as each car went up and down the road, but James never turned the doorknob. Breakfast was quiet. Ralph poured himself a glass of orange juice. "Momma, where's daddy?" asked Charlotte. We haven't seen him all week." Jake was waiting to hear what Roxie was going to say, but she remained silent. She still had not thought about what she was going to tell the children. Roxie feared the truth would confirm the rumors that Charlotte heard at Judy's party. Ralph abruptly stormed out of the kitchen leaving his breakfast untouched. "I don't have an appetite," he said. Ralph didn't know where his father was, but he had a good idea of why he wasn't home with them. Roxie took a deep breath and explained to Charlotte and Jake that James would not be coming back. Charlotte asked why and Roxie responded, "Your father has moved on and we'll just have to get along without him now." Weeks passed, then months and no sign of James. Roxie had to go to work full time to make ends meet. She and James never legally divorced they just stayed separated.

Several years had passed, and no one had seen or heard from James. Roxie made ends meet the best way she could, taking on a full-time shift at the sewing factory.

It was a beautiful Saturday morning in May. Roxie was making sure there were no hanging threads left on the satin teal-green prom dress that she had made for Charlotte. There was a knock at the door. "Come in!" yelled Roxie, from down the hall. She didn't know who it could be, she wasn't expecting any guests. When Roxie came up the hall, James was standing there looking thin and frail. From the way things looked, walking away from his family was harder on him than Roxie. James had taken up a hobby of drinking and lost his jobs at the Steel Manufacturing Company and the bakery. James was also a diabetic and his health had declined so much that he had to move back home with his parents. Jake was almost as tall as James now but most of the memories he had of James had dimmed.

Roxie didn't know what to say. For years, she had been dismissing the guilt of her actions with Charlie but for the first time, she was standing face to face with the grim manifestation of her selfish actions. "Is that you daddy?" asked Charlotte, walking up the hall in her prom dress. "Roxie, she's just as pretty as you," said James. Charlotte ran over to hug her father, but she pulled away slowly because he wreaked of cigarette-smoke and alcohol. James also had an uncontrollable sway. Charlotte had never seen her father drunk before. Prior to this moment, Charlotte had a lot of questions for her father, but now, she didn't know if he had the mental capacity to answer anything she wanted to know. Jake just sat on the sofa catching up on his Saturday morning cartoons. He always felt his father was somewhat distant towards him before he left, but Jake didn't feel the need to bond with James anymore, especially after he abandoned them.

James looked at Jake sitting on the sofa. "You don't remember me," he asked? Roxie interrupted, "You left, and didn't have anything else to do with your own children. Why would you want them to remember you?" Roxie was trying to make James feel guilty, while at the same time, creating an excuse for having that lazy "Jimmy" hanging around the house, her latest boyfriend, who was in the bedroom asleep. When Roxie needed Charlie's help, he was nowhere to be found. Jimmy would stay with Roxie until she threatened to put him out, then he would go back to his mother's house and sleep on the sofa. James sensed the children were upset with him. He didn't want to disgrace Roxie, even though he suspected she had told them her tainted version of why he left. James left and never returned, leaving it up to the children to visit him at his parent's house, if they want to see him. Besides, he couldn't stand the thought of coming over, while Roxie had another man in the house. I don't know if James ever got over Roxie.

# 18

## THE ACCIDENT

A few weeks after James's visit, Roxie boxed up all of Jimmy's belongings and put them beside the road. Out with Jimmy and in with Billy. Billy was married, but he told Roxie that he was leaving his wife, Janey. Unlike Jimmy, he could keep a job and he gave Roxie money from time to time. Sometimes, James would walk away from his parent's house into the yard to smoke a cigarette and he would look down the hill and see Billy coming over to Roxie's house. James would put his cigarette out and go back inside the house. James's health continued to decline, his diabetes became so severe, that he slipped into a diabetic coma twice... while living with his parents.

Roxie worked from 6:00 a.m. to 2:30 p.m. She was always tired when she got off work but that didn't mean her shift had ended. Roxie still had to prepare dinner and meet Jake at the top of the road after school.

We had gotten off the bus one afternoon. Ron and I walked to our apartment, Matt, Spencer, and Laura walked with Jake, until they got to their house. Jake continued walking by himself, but he didn't see Roxie on foot or in her car. Roxie was at home lying on the sofa with Billy, it had completely slipped her mind that it was time to meet Jake. As Jake walked home, his thoughts were perplexed. He didn't have a relationship with his father and his mother was starting to confirm everything his grandfather had told him about women. Jake bent down to pick up some rocks along the edge of the road to see how far he could throw them. When Jake stood up, he stepped back onto the road. A car was coming over the hill traveling too fast. When the driver noticed Jake, he couldn't stop in time. The car hit Jake, knocking him into the air. Jake landed on the road and his book bag went into the ditch. The driver panicked as he got out of the car to see about him.

Bam! Bam! Bam! Roxie got up and went to the door as the knocking shook fear into her heart. Somebody in their neighborhood was passing by and recognized Jake laying in the road and drove to Roxie's house to tell her what had happened. By the time she got to the top of the road, the

EMT's had strapped Jake to a stretcher, loaded him inside the back of the ambulance, and was taking him to the hospital. Jake was scared and in a lot of pain. He had never been taken anywhere without his mother before. He wanted Roxie to come with him, but she didn't make it in time. Roxie ran back to the house to get her purse and the car. Jake had several broken bones and had suffered a mild concussion. The doctors bandaged him up and put casts on both of his arms and one of his legs. When Jake woke up, he didn't want Roxie to leave his side, but she had to go home and get ready for work the next day. She knew Jake's medication would be kicking in again soon. Roxie promised to visit him on her lunch break, and she would come back when she got off work. When Roxie returned home that evening, she turned around to close the door and noticed Virginia peering at her and shaking her head from her porch. Roxie closed the door slowly and thought to herself, no words could have been more painful than the look on Virginia's face.

Roxie didn't see Billy anymore, she had a pang of overwhelming guilt that if she had not been with him, Jake would not be in the hospital. As time went on, Jake became stronger each day. When Roxie went to visit him, she would walk along-side his wheelchair as the nurse pushed him down to see the physical therapist. Jake would soon be released to go home, but he still had a long way to recovery, and he needed someone to be with him all day. Roxie had to stop working at the sewing company and she was able to get a job working the night shift at Shady Oakes Retirement Home for Senior Living. Ralph would help at night if Jake needed anything and Roxie tended to him when she came home from work in the morning between naps. Charlotte was too consumed with herself to help, she had become quite the flirt and was very popular with the guys. Charlotte's beauty caused her to have a lot of enemies though, as she often flirted with the guys who had girlfriends.

We missed Jake walking to and from school with us. We even missed all his rules and clarifications on the football field. While Jake was at home recovering, Matt and I were still coping with the cards that life dealt us each day.

# 19

## A BUMP IN THE ROAD

One day after school, Matt was in the kitchen fixing Spencer and Laura's snack before Marie came home from work. Matt heard the rattling of keys and laughter at the door - Marie opened the front door, she had groceries in one arm and her purse in the other. Matt ran to help her with the groceries, but he was instantly paralyzed in his tracks. There stood a tall stranger behind Marie with two more bags of groceries. Matt didn't know what to think. "Matt, I want you to meet Len and Len... I want you to meet Matt," said Marie. "Matt is the little man that helps me out so much around here. I don't know what I would do without him." Marie walked past Matt to the kitchen and put the grocery bags on the table. Len followed her, but Matt was still standing at the front door... holding it wide open. Matt was staring at Len, trying to figure out where Marie met him, and how long he would stick around. Len was unshaven, he had on a blue uniform that was soiled with dirt and grease. The leather on his boots was torn at the toe, revealing the steel toe underneath. Matt finally closed the door and went to his room to take in what he had just observed. "Matt," yelled Marie. Matt didn't hear her the first time, so she yelled again, "Matt." When Matt snapped out of his thoughts, he could hear Marie asking, "Where is your brother and sister?" "Oh, they're in your room watching cartoons," Matt yelled from his bedroom. "Well, tell them to come here, I want them to meet Len, he's having dinner with us tonight."

Dinner was quiet, Marie and Len giggled at each other, but nobody knew what was funny but them. After dinner, Matt was the first to get up from the table to get a bath and get ready for bed. Marie didn't even notice that he had left the table. She gave Spencer and Laura baths and got them ready for bed, while Len entertained himself in the living room, watching TV. Later that night Matt lay awake, listening to hear Len crank up and leave, but he never heard an engine turn on. Matt got out of bed and looked out the window to see what kind of car Len drove, but he only saw Marie's station wagon. That's odd, he thought, maybe he already left. Matt turned over and eventually fell asleep but was later awakened by the same giggling that ruined his dinner. Not again, he thought to himself. This was bad, Len didn't even have his own car. Was this the best she could do? Matt knew this was going to be a long night as he struggled to zone out the sounds coming from Marie's room and the racing thoughts in his mind.

The next morning, Marie was up early fixing breakfast, but the door to her room was still closed. Matt asked Marie if Len spent the night. Marie paused and said, "Yes he did, Why?" In a slightly tempered voice, Matt asked, "Is he going to be spending the night here all the time?" Marie sensed that Matt wasn't fond of Len. "Momma, where did you meet this guy and how long have you known him?" asked Matt. Marie paused and said, "Just give him a chance, he's really a nice guy. Matt grabbed his briefcase and stormed out the door to catch up with me, leaving Spencer and Laura with Marie.

On the way to school, Matt didn't have much to say. I asked him if he was all right, but he just looked down at the ground and kept walking. Whatever was going on, it was serious. Matt had always been a deep thinker, but he never held grudges against people for long.

Len and Marie never married. Sometimes Len would spend the night, and other times, he wouldn't...but in between those intervals, Marie became pregnant. Len stuck around for a little while. After she gave birth to a little girl named April, Len started coming around less and less. Usually, he would have somebody bring him over once a month when he knew Matt would be home and Marie would still be at work. Len would knock on the door. When Matt opened it, Len would be standing there with a bag of pampers and he would say," "What's up little man? Can you give these to your mother, and tell her I dropped by?" Matt wouldn't respond, he would grab the bag, close the door, and go back to watching Spencer and Laura. April would still be at the babysitter's house. After April turned a year old, Len stopped coming around altogether.

Three years had passed, and Matt was 14 years old. Marie had started secretly seeing a guy named Derrick for a while before she introduced him to Matt. When she finally brought Derrick around, he appeared to be very friendly, but Matt could see right through him. It wasn't long before they found out Derrick was a heavy drinker, and he harbored a dark secret that would soon come to light. Whenever Derrick consumed too much alcohol, he became very angry. Derrick grew up in a violent household, he almost killed his stepfather for fighting his mother. Matt knew Derrick was trouble - the first time he walked in the door, just like all the previous guys his mother dated. Matt didn't trust Derrick and he was scared for Marie to be alone with him. As usual, Matt had a hard time sleeping with a strange man in the house, but he knew he had school the next day.

Matt was tired from tossing and turning all night, but he got up and went to school anyway. He had a hard time focusing during class the whole day. Finally, the afternoon bell rang. Matt could pack up and go home.

James and Robert were two guys that fought almost every day after school, not because they wanted to, but because everybody pressured them to. Today, they were going to meet up on the path behind the apartments - as usual. Matt would usually try to talk them out of it if he could catch them before the fight started but today, he had a lot on his mind, and he had a feeling that he should get home right away. I think James was more afraid of Robert, but his fear of being deemed a coward kept him from declining the fight. If anybody asked either of them if they were going to fight after school, they would say yes, and a crowd would show up to see what was going to happen.

It was 4 o'clock in the afternoon, in a cloud of dust, James and Robert were locked arm in arm. Robert kicked his leg under James's leg, causing him to fall to the ground and Robert took the advantage to climb on top of James and punch him in the face. James had a bloody nose, and everybody circled around them, cheering for Robert. Suddenly, James reached over and grabbed a large rock and hit Robert in the side of the head. Instantly, Robert fell over to the ground as if he had been shot. At first, everybody cheered for Robert to get back up and finish the fight, but once they realized he wasn't moving, somebody said, "He's not moving!" "Is he dead?" asked Kenneth. "I don't know," said Sheryl, "This doesn't look good and I'm getting out of here." Everybody started running. Robert had fallen over, but his legs were still straddled over James. James shoved Robert completely off him. He grabbed his book bag and staggered all the way home. Robert had died from trauma blunt force to the head. Matt and I had already started walking home ahead of the crowd because we didn't want to take part in any of it. Out of nowhere, a flood of our classmates came running past us. We didn't know what was going on. Kenneth stopped long enough to tell us what had just happened. We felt horrible, Matt was extremely torn up over the situation. I knew exactly what he was thinking. He believed he could have prevented it, if only he had stopped thinking about his own problems long enough to talk to them. "There was nothing you could have done Matt, you talked to those fools every day. I hate to say it, but it was bound to happen one day. They wouldn't listen," I told him. I could tell the talk made Matt feel a little better, but that would not be the last battle he would encounter before the day was over.

Just like every other day, it was time for us to go our separate ways. Ron and I had become clever at sneaking through the apartments and avoiding the gangs. Matt waited at the bus stop for Spencer and Laura's bus to arrive. As soon as Laura stepped off the bus, she said, "Look, Matt." She had pieces of colored construction paper glued to another piece of paper in the shape of a butterfly." She couldn't wait to hear what Matt had to say about it. "That's beautiful Laura." Jacob pulled a rock out of his pocket that he had found on the playground and showed it to Matt. It was a piece of white quartz. Along with the foreboding feeling Matt had in his stomach, he suddenly felt emptiness for Spencer and Laura. Their father would never see their faces light up as he did, he wouldn't know how artistic Laura was, or how much Spencer loved Science.

As they approached the yard, Matt was glad to see Marie's car in the driveway. When Marie graduated from Culinary School, she was able to quit working at the bakery and start her own catering business. Spencer and Laura's constant jibber-jabber had turned into one combined sound that had no meaning. Matt had zoned them out because he sensed something was wrong as soon as he stepped onto the yard. When they arrived at the front door, he could hear a male voice yelling from inside the house. When Matt opened the door, there stood Derrick, already drunk with his hands raised over his head yelling at Marie. She had her head down continuing to nervously frost a cake that she was making for a client. Derrick had gotten angry because she was ignoring him, so he slapped the cake off the table and then he shoved Marie against the wall. Matt laid his briefcase down, rushed his little brother and sister down the hall to Marie's bedroom, and pulled the door closed. He told Spencer to turn on their favorite cartoons. Matt went back up the hall to see about Marie, then he ran through the kitchen and grabbed a shovel from the carport. Matt was tall for a 14-year-old. He hit Derrick in the back with the shovel and Derrick went stumbling forward. "Now get out and don't come back," yelled Matt. Derrick turned and looked at him in a drunken stupor. Matt went to stand in front of Marie with the shovel. Derrick staggered for a minute then grabbed his keys off the living room table and went out the front door to his truck. He swerved out of the yard and that was the last time they saw Derrick.

Marie went to the bathroom. She was crying and vomiting. Matt thought she was just upset over the situation, but she was pregnant again. A new baby was going to add financial strain, but Marie never bothered to reach out to Derrick, she just went on with her life.

# 20

## HOPE DEFERRED

We were 16 now, Jake had fully recovered, and was playing football with us again. I was growing facial hair, becoming muscular like my father, and my voice had deepened. Unfortunately, I was nowhere near as intimidating as I looked. In fact, I was quite sensitive. Puberty wasn't kind to me, as my face was scarred with acne. The kids at school were brutal, but I pretended like it didn't bother me - just like all the slaps I got at home. I was good at hiding my emotions and making excuses for my random collection of bruises. When I was by myself, I would let the tears flow. Lena was still confined to the house by Momma. As the years went by, Lena and Momma continued to take their frustrations out on me with shoes, pans, or whatever they could get their hands on. The physical and verbal abuse took a toll on my masculinity overtime - as my grades and self- esteem continued to suffer as well.

One day, I was going to run across the street to Ms. Shirley's apartment to get some chips and a soda. When I got downstairs, I heard someone giggling to my right. It was Jessica and Lyndsey, the two sisters next door. Jessica was 16 and Lyndsey was 17. They were on the front porch making bracelets with colored string and beads. What they were doing looked interesting and I wanted to join them, but if the guys caught me playing with them, I wouldn't have to worry about Lena and Momma anymore, the guys would kill me. I waved at them and proceeded to walk over to Ms. Shirley's apartment, she was already watching me out of the window. After I returned to our apartment, I remembered I was supposed to be going down to Sam's Stop N' Shop to apply for the job that was posted in the window. I changed my clothes and hurried down to Sam's store.

When I arrived, the shelf-stocking job had been filled, but a bagger had quit, so Sam hired me to bag groceries and load them into the customer's cars. I worked three days a week after school, and every other Saturday. I had a change jar under my bed where I put all the tips I earned. Uncle Daniel opened a savings account for me to deposit my checks and I would be getting my driver's license soon.

Early Saturday morning, I was up at 8:00. I didn't have to work, but there was no sleeping in late…, if Momma was home, she didn't care if you were tired or not. Usually, she had her friends over twice a month, and she would serve brunch – compliments of Lena and Aunt Liz. She made sure that I cleaned up after they left- washing the dishes, sweeping, and mopping the floor. Lena had gone to town with Aunt Liz. Ron was good at getting out of chores, he would disappear with his friends before anybody could make him do anything. I ate a bowl of Toasty Flakes and put my jacket on and headed towards the door.  Momma said, "You better be back here soon so you can wash the dishes when my guests leave." I didn't say anything, I pulled the door closed behind me and ran over to the field to see where Matt and Jake were. Today was a beautiful day and everybody was on the field. I could see Jake telling everybody what to do as I got closer. "What's up, Timothy?" Matt hi-fived me. "Where have you been bro?" "Well, I got a job at Sam's Stop N' Shop after school, and I'm off this Saturday." I had not seen the guys in two weeks. We didn't have any classes or lunch together this year. It seemed like we played football all day to make up for the time we missed. Jake scored two touchdowns but whenever he was tackled or dropped the ball, he blamed it on the fact that his arm had been broken a few years ago. I had two touch downs. Our team could have done better if Matt had not been so careful not to hurt anyone. After a while, the teams started dwindling down as everybody had other things to do that afternoon.

After the football game, Me, Jake, and Matt headed over to the drug store. Linda's strawberry blonde hair had turned white, but she still had the same hairstyle, pasty white skin, red lipstick, and the addition of a few crow's feet around the edges of her eyes. No matter how long we stayed away, Linda always remembered us. She would put her plastic gloves on and start dispensing the soda into the glasses and scooping the chocolate ice cream as soon as she saw us walk in the door. After Linda finished making our chocolate ice cream sodas, we sat outside on the bench and talked about what was going on in our lives. We laughed and talked about the game and all of Jake's excuses for messing up. I thought I was the only one who had a real job now, but apparently, Matt and Jake had also gotten better-paying jobs to help their families at home. Jake was stocking inventory at the clothing outlet store and Matt did construction work with his uncle. Jake told how his mother had been struggling since his father walked out on them.

"But it's all right, karma got him," he said. "He can't even take care of himself now, and he's on disability." Then he looked at me and said, "Hey Timothy, you still getting beat up by your grandmother?" "Nah," I said, "She's calmed down a lot, but I knew that was far from the truth." Matt was very secretive. He didn't have much to say other than the guys that his mother dated didn't deserve her and that she was too good of a woman for them.

All the way home, I was thinking about all the fun I had with the guys today. I guess it was just a lucky coincidence that we were all there on the same day. Today was a good day. I can't remember the last time I laughed so much. I was tired and full of chocolate ice cream soda. By the time I reached the top step of our apartment and opened the door, Momma grabbed me by the collar with her fist clenched, snatching me inside. I glanced to see if anybody was watching, as I tried to make it appear that I stumbled into the doorway. Even though I had blue jeans on, I could feel each painful welt stinging and swelling from the broom handle. "I told you I was having guests over today, and you had better be back here in time to wash those dishes when we got finished!" she said. I didn't say a word and I held back every tear - knowing that one day, I was getting out of there. Ron was at Tony's house. Lena always had somewhere for him to go, so he didn't have to spend as much time with Momma as I did. When I finished washing the dishes, I went to my room and laid down and went to sleep.

I woke to Lena sticking her head in my room saying, "Boy, get out there and get those bags out of the car." I raised up and sat on the side of my bunk bed, resting my forehead in the palm of my hands. "How did a day that started so well, end so badly?" I let out a deep breath, put my shoes on, and headed out of the door and down the steps to get the bags out of Aunt Liz's trunk. By that time, Ron came walking up with Tony - as if he was somewhere waiting for Lena to return home. Ron knew that if I was getting bags out of the car, Lena must have gotten something for him. He didn't help get the bags in, he just ran up the steps and started rummaging through them, looking for something sweet, which explains why he was so overweight. Lena spoiled him with everything he wanted. Ron didn't have to work like I did, Lena always gave him spending money. I would try to get him to come and play football with me and my friends, but he preferred to watch TV and eat junk food at Tony's, who was also overweight.

I didn't tell Lena about Momma, when I finished

getting the bags out of the car. It seemed as if they were allies against me. Whenever Momma complained about me, Lena just agreed with her.

Sunday morning, I was sitting in the living room, reading the comic section of the newspaper. For whatever reason, Lena really didn't care if I didn't go to church anymore. A minute away from Momma, was a minute that I enjoyed. As I was turning to the sports article, Lena came strutting up the hall, she was wearing a fitted mint green dress with a green sequence belt, coffee tinted stockings, mint green high hills, and a green sequence hat. As I lowered the newspaper to get a good look at her, she rubbed her hands down her sides and around to the back of her bottom - as if she was ironing the dress onto her body with the palms of her hands. At that moment, I was taken back to when I was a little boy, and she would model her dresses for me. As I began to smile, the trauma from the years between then and now began to subside. Out of nowhere, Wham! I felt the sting of cold leather on the side of my face. "You don't sit there and gaze at your mother like that!" Momma struck me with her bible. Before I knew it, I had jumped up and drawn my fist back to hit her and I felt Lena restraining my arm behind me and saying, "You can't hit your grandmother, what's wrong with you boy?" I knew that moment, it was time for me to get out of that apartment. I just couldn't take it anymore. I snatched away from Lena, went to my room, and laid across my bed. A few minutes later, I heard the front door close. Momma and Lena went to church while Aunt Liz stayed home to start Sunday dinner.

I slept the whole time they were gone. I woke to the voice of Momma, Lena, and several other men talking. I could smell baked barbecue ribs, cornbread, macaroni and cheese, and candied yams. I sat on the side of my bed to see if I could make out who was talking, then I went up the hall and peered around the corner. It was Reverend North, Deacon Whitaker, and Deacon Mobley. I went back down the hall because the children were not allowed to eat while the clergy were eating. This was the only time Lena could be in the presence of a man and not have Momma get upset with her. Deacon Whitaker and Deacon Mobley were around Lena's age and Reverend North was around Momma's age. I couldn't figure out why they couldn't eat at home with their wives or why they never came with them. Aunt Liz and Lena would prepare a spread for them - as if they were Royalty. Momma would even prepare her cream cheese pound cake the night before. When I heard Reverend North complimenting Aunt Liz for the food, I knew they were getting ready to leave. Me, Ron, and Cindy could come and get something to eat now. Out of the corner of my eye, I saw the tail end of Deacon Whitaker's jacket leaving out of the front door, then his hand reached back in and grabbed Lena's hand. He whispered something in her ear and kissed her on the cheek.

When Monday morning came, I thought to myself, what a weekend. I didn't feel like going to school or anywhere else. I got dressed, went downstairs, and cut through the path behind the apartments. I walked until I got out of sight, to make Momma think I was gone to school, but I went to the pool hall to hang out. The guys and I didn't meet up every morning like we use to. Some days, Matt would stay out of school to work and help his mother with the living expenses at home.

I missed one day of school, then another and another. Before I knew it, I had not been to school in two weeks. I always made sure to leave the pool hall in time to get back before Lena got home from work.

One afternoon, Lena called me in the kitchen, she had an envelope in her hand. "This letter says you have 10 consecutive school absences." I didn't say anything, I was tired…tired of life. "You go to school or you get out!" said

Lena.

That night, Lena called my Uncle Leonard in Mississippi and told him what was going on with me. Uncle Leonard agreed to let me move to Mississippi with him and my grandmother so I could finish high school. My birthday was in August, so I would graduate at age 17. Uncle Leonard and Grandma seemed happy to have me there. Uncle Leonard had a son named Antwon who was 15 years old. He was the only grandchild in Mississippi, and he could do no wrong in my grandmother's eyes. Antwon's mother wasn't ready to be a mother, so she gave Uncle Leonard custody of him when he was born, and she went on with her life. Antwon had been raised by Uncle Leonard and Grandma ever since. Something I noticed about Antwon immediately was that he was spoiled - just like Ron, back at home.

One day, I was playing basketball with Antwon and some of his friends. Antwon kept making illegal moves on the court, fouling, and carrying the ball. Jeff told Antwon to stop cheating and Antwon got mad and shoved him. Jeff jumped on Antwon. When we got home Antwon's right cheek was bruised. He told my grandmother the guys were bullying him on the basketball court, and I wouldn't take up for him. My grandmother scolded me, I got a bath and went to my room. I didn't even bother to defend myself and tell her that Antwon started the fight, I don't think it would have mattered anyway. I tossed and turned all night long. The next morning, I called Lena and told her what happened. She feared that I wouldn't make it there either, so I just moved back home. I packed my belongings and Uncle Daniel came and picked me up that Saturday morning. When we arrived at the apartment, Momma was the first person that I saw. It wasn't like her to be without words but surprisingly, she didn't have anything to say.

Saturday afternoon, I was in front of one of the guy's apartments that I met at the pool hall. They were older than me and most of them had already dropped out of school and started working. They weren't the best people to hang around, but they accepted me, and it always felt good to belong. They were glad to see me back at home and asked where had I been. I explained to them that I had moved away for a little while. They asked if I wanted a beer. I said, "Yeah." Lena saw me through the window. She raised the window and told me to come here. I gave the bottle of beer back as if it wasn't mine. I was good at playing things off in front of my friends, especially when I was in trouble. "We didn't get you in trouble, did we?" they asked. "No…I'll catch up with ya'll later," I said.

When I got inside the apartment, Lena said, "Did I see you out there drinking?" I lied and said, "No." "I told you that you weren't going to amount to anything, just like your father." I just stood there looking like I didn't care, because I didn't care about anything anymore. By that time, Momma was making her way towards me. Uncle Daniel got up from the sofa to get me away from Lena and Momma and he started yelling, "This boy won't ever become a man because of ya'll! Lena, you confused him at an early age, and you know what I'm talking about. You send him to the store where all his classmates hang out to buy your feminine products, ya'll beat him and tear him down with your words every day. It's a wonder that he's not a lot worse-off than what he is!" Uncle Daniel walked me down the hall so he could talk to me. "Boy, don't you let these women strip you of your manhood. Finish school, so you can make something of yourself. Momma has been bitter ever since daddy died, and your momma is becoming just like her. If you finish school, you can get out of here and never have to look back!"

# 21

## A NEW HOPE

Early Saturday morning, I heard a knock at the door, it was my mother's oldest brother's son, Cousin Lee. He came to ask Lena for a favor. He wanted to know if she would co-sign with him to get a new car and loan him the money for a down payment. All my cousins thought Lena was everything. She was their favorite aunt and she never said no to them. Lena went down-town to get the money out of the bank, then to the dealership to help Lee purchase his first car. While Ron and I waited at the bus stop in the mornings, he would pass us in his 75' Monte Carlo.

Before I moved to Mississippi with my grandmother, I told Sam I had to leave for a little while, but I didn't tell him why. I was a good worker prior to leaving and when I returned, he gave me my old job back. There was a car that I liked at a used car dealership, downtown. I had saved enough money to make a decent down payment, but I needed a co-signer, since I didn't have any credit. That night, I waited for Lena to come home. I told her about the car, and she said, "You can't get a car, you need insurance." I told her I could work and pay for my own insurance each month. "What did I say?" she replied, then she went into her room and closed the door. I don't think I got any sleep that night.

The next day, I woke up before my alarm clock went off, I still had to wake Ron. We got ready for school, Lena had already left for work, and Cindy caught a ride with Mandy's mother to the bus stop. I had a good feeling, I didn't know why, but I just felt it in my bones. Ron met Tony outside, and I ran to see if Matt and Jake were at the bus stop. When we got to school, I noticed there were guys in neat uniforms walking around the cafeteria. I was so curious that I couldn't eat my breakfast. These guys had booths set up on the stage and each of them represented a different branch of the United States Military. An Army officer came to shake our hand and talk to us about joining and taking the ASVAB. We listened attentively. Jake didn't know what he wanted to do after high school. Matt wanted to go to college, but he had too many oppositions at the time. I wasn't sure about what I wanted to do either, but anything that would get me out of the house with Momma and Lena sounded good. I told the officer that I was interested in signing up for the Army. I shook his hand and he said he would schedule a day and time for me to stop by his recruitment office to take the written exam. I thought to myself, I knew there was a reason why I felt so good when I got up this morning.

Two weeks later, I scored a B on the exam. For the first time, I understood what was on test, unlike the ones I took in school. A few days later, the recruiter scheduled me to take a physical exam and I graduated from high school in June.

Each day, I waited with anticipation for my acceptance letter to come in the mail, and finally, it came. I couldn't wait to show it to Uncle Daniel. He hugged me so tight and congratulated me. We agreed to keep it a secret. That night, I couldn't sleep, and this time, it was for a good reason.

During our high school graduation, Jake had a lot of hands patting him on the back as he received his mock diploma and walked across the stage. Honestly, I don't know if the faculty were congratulating him, or rushing him to get off the stage before he got any ideas about grabbing the microphone and saying something.

Matt didn't graduate when we did. Working to help his mother take care of his siblings, caused him to fall behind in school. A year later, he earned his GED.

Two weeks after my graduation, the apartment was quiet. Lena was fixing Momma something to eat, I was in my room, Aunt Liz was watching TV, and Uncle Daniel was reading the newspaper. There was a knock at the door. Uncle Daniel got up from the sofa in the living room to see who it was. The officer introduced himself and shook his hand. Momma yelled from the kitchen, "Who is that Daniel?" He didn't respond, he just invited the officer in and yelled down the hall to let me know my ride was there. Momma and Lena came out of the kitchen and stared with their mouths open. Everything appeared to be in slow motion. Aunt Liz stood up to see what was going on as I came up the hall with my bags packed. When I got to the front door, Uncle Daniel gave me a hug and said, "Take care of yourself, you hear?" He knew I had to go so he didn't keep me any longer. Nobody else in the apartment said a word. I pulled the door closed behind me and left behind the officer. I assumed Lena told Ron and Cindy where I had gone when they came home from their friend's houses.

Day 1 of boot camp: I was 17 years old and was now enlisted in the United States Army and stationed in South Carolina for training. I had an idea of what Bootcamp consisted of but unlike most people, my PTSD started prior to entering the military. I was hypervigilant and always looking over my shoulders. Having ammunition going off all the time didn't help either. The first couple of nights, I had nightmares. Early one morning, I dreamed Momma was very angry with me and she was screaming my name, but when I woke up, it was Sergeant Peterson, hollering for us to get up for running drills.

I remembered Matt saying, "There's nothing you can't pray about." I prayed for God to help me make it through boot camp. Going to Chapel gave me encouragement as well.

I persevered through bootcamp and finally, graduation day came. No one came to my graduation, but I didn't care, I was glad to make it through basic training. The rest of my time in the military was not as stressful. I traveled and learned a lot, but I couldn't wait to get out. Nearly 4 ½ years later, I was honorably discharged from the United States Army.

# 22

## COMING OF AGE

During the time I was in the Army, Matt continued to work and help Marie. He spent many nights praying for his family and studying his bible when everybody went to sleep. Matt was able to understand the weight of poverty and responsibility at an early age and he was no stranger to hard work.

One afternoon, Marie was at home preparing cornbread, crowder peas, and fried chicken for dinner. Matt had gotten in a habit of doing nice things for his mother because he knew it made her happy. In between jobs, he would purchase Marie a bouquet of flowers; living up to the title of being the "Little Man" around the house, yet still deprived of his childhood. Matt continued to buy himself nice clothes whenever he could. Even though his photo was seldom in the yearbook due to his many absences, it wasn't uncommon for our classmates to borrow his clothes on picture day. Matt was always thinking ahead, he knew that his brothers and sisters would be entering college before long and Marie would need him to help. Matt figured that he and Marie could put a little bit of money aside for each of them, and that would give them a head start. They would eventually have to get jobs of their own to pay their tuition. Matt was respected by his younger siblings, they looked up to him as he was the only father figure they knew. When things around the house tore up, such as the appliances or the car, Marie could always depend on Matt. Working two jobs for a while now, he was hoping that Marie was becoming more financially stable. Matt was becoming a man and he was ready to accept his Ministerial calling and would eventually start a family of his own one day.

Jake started working for Wade's Concrete with Ralph. Ralph was back and forth at home, as his first marriage was annulled and the second one just didn't work out. Charlotte moved to the city as soon as she finished high school. She loved the fast life and only came to visit during the holidays. Charlotte would arrive in extravagant attire, with her expensive perfume, and jewelry. Her managerial position at the fancy hotel downtown Birmingham paid her a decent wage, but not enough to afford her lavish lifestyle.

It was assumed that her many admirers showered her with expensive gifts, as she always showed up with a different gentleman on her arm.

Jake's car accident brought him and Roxie closer than ever and now that he has grown up, he seems to be more responsible than either of his siblings. Roxie always referred to him as the "Little Man of the House." When Jake started working at Wade's Concrete, Roxie didn't have to work near as hard as she did when he was younger. No matter how tired Jake was, when he came in from pouring concrete all day, he always had time to stop by Roxie's room to make sure she was all right and he would ask if she needed anything.

Roxie had not been feeling well for a few days, so Jake took her to the hospital. After having some tests run, they found that she was having heart failure. Roxie was scheduled to undergo coronary artery bypass surgery. Jake visited her while she was in the hospital and picked her up when she was released. Jake grew up seeing how hard Roxie struggled after James left, and he hated to see how men took advantage of his mother. He wanted to relieve her from having to accept whatever handouts they felt like giving her.

The house that Jake and Roxie were currently living in

needed a lot of work and the plumbing issues would require a considerable amount of money. Jake didn't want to add any more stress to Roxie, so he took it upon himself to look for some property on the country side of town and build them a quaint home. He was able to find the perfect location. When Roxie started feeling better, Jake took her to see the property, then he showed her the floor plan that he had a contractor design. Roxie was so happy. This would be her forever home. About six months later, they were packing up and moving in. Roxie never missed an opportunity to praise Jake, just as he suspected she would. Jake worked so much that when he was home, he was usually resting, but everything was going well.

Late one afternoon, Jake was driving home from work. He was tired as usual. As he approached his new house, he noticed there was a car parked on his side of the driveway and it wasn't Ralph's. Jake had to park behind Roxie's car so he wouldn't block them in when they got ready to leave. He thought to himself, maybe Roxie had a guest over. When Jake got his lunch box out of his truck and walked inside the house, he noticed that it was very quiet. He didn't hear the TV or any conversation going on. Jake walked into the kitchen and looked around, then he went down the hall to check on Roxie. When he got to her door, it was locked. Jake knocked on the door and said, "Momma." Roxie responded, "I'll be out in a minute." Jake went to his room and a few minutes later he heard Roxie's door open. Jake wanted to see who was leaving her room, so he stuck his head out of his bedroom door. A girthy, rough-looking guy with a few teeth came stepping out of her room, adjusting his britches. The image that Jake saw bothered him. He had not anticipated useless men in the new house that he was working hard to pay for, especially the kind that didn't have the decency to acknowledge him as the man of the house or come around when his mother needed taken care of.

Jake started dating a young lady named Laverne Styles, trying to put Roxie's male friends as far from his mind as possible. Laverne was a Christian, but that didn't keep Jake from dating her. Laverne was pretty, kind, and smart. She could cook very well but cooking and cleaning wasn't something she cared to do often. Laverne's career was more important than being a homemaker, but she loved Jake. Unfortunately, Jake had begun to view all women through the model Roxie had set, causing him to misinterpret the better qualities that Laverne possessed.

One night around 11:00, there was a knock at the door. Everybody heard the knock, but when Roxie and Jake heard Ralph getting up, they laid silently in their beds to hear who it was. Ralph walked up the hall and peered out the window. When he saw it was Charlotte, he opened the door to let her in. Charlotte didn't say anything, she just grabbed her luggage off the front porch and made her way inside the house. Ralph locked the door behind her and went back to bed, without turning on any lights. Roxie crashed on the sofa and stayed there all night. Jake and Roxie heard the commotion. "Who is it Ralph?" yelled Roxie. "It's Charlotte," he replied. Ralph and Jake went back to sleep. Roxie had to be at work early in the morning, so she decided to talk to Charlotte before she left out.

The next morning, Roxie got up to go to work, she noticed Charlotte on the sofa, so she woke her up to talk to her. Charlotte wreaked of alcohol and she looked a mess, Roxie couldn't get a clear understanding of her murmurs, so she decided to talk to her after she got home from work. Jake may have been Roxie's safety net, but Charlotte had always been her favorite and she always held the most delicate place in her heart.

When Jake got ready for work, he saw Charlotte lying on the sofa. The fast life must have finally caught up with her, he thought, as he walked out the door. That was Jake's sister, but he knew she had some conniving ways, especially, when it came to getting what she wanted. Jake had no idea that Charlotte had picked up a habit while she was in the city that would change life as he knew it forever.

When Roxie came home, she found Charlotte clearing a space for herself and her things in a corner of the basement. She didn't know how long Charlotte would be there, and before she could ask, Charlotte told her she just needed to stay there - long enough to get back on her feet. She had lost her job and her apartment. Roxie didn't question anything Charlotte said, she told her she could stay there as long as she needed. Charlotte's beauty had diminished tremendously, her long thick hair was thinning, her skin had sores, and her teeth were chipped and discolored.

Charlotte had been living with them for about three months now, and Jake was still working long hours and paying most of the bills. This Saturday would be his first day off in a while. Jake got up early so he could go to the bank before Laverne came over. When Jake arrived at the bank, he asked the teller for an account balance. Usually, Jake would take time to embellish in the rewards of his labor, but when he saw what was printed on the receipt, he was furious. Jake was missing two thousand dollars and he wanted to know why. The teller pulled his previous transactions which were multiple checks written out to cash. He didn't even have to think about who it could have been. After going back and forth with the teller and the bank manager about pressing charges, Jake had a secure lock put on his account, and he stormed out of the bank.

When Jake got home, he jumped out of his old pick-up and ran inside the house, looking for Charlotte in a rage. Roxie came to the front room to see what was going on. "I went to the bank today and a couple thousand dollars were missing from my account!" yelled Jake. "They wanted me to press charges against the individual after an investigation, but I knew it was Charlotte! Apparently, she stole my checkbook out of my room, while I was at work!" All Roxie could say was, "I'm glad you didn't turn your own sister in to the police." Jake could not believe what Roxie had just said, as if she could have cared less about Charlotte stealing his money. The only thing that mattered to Roxie at that moment was the safety of Charlotte. "Charlotte is having a hard time right now," said Roxie. "You should never have let her come here! She's on drugs, and she's not going to stop stealing until everything in this house is missing!" Charlotte was in the bathroom and she could hear Jake yelling, but when she came out of the bathroom, she was slightly out of it. Jake got in his truck and went to the hardware store to purchase a new lock for his bedroom door.

Charlotte was forced to find a new source of income to supply her habit. Sometimes, Laverne would come over before Jake would get home from work, she would wait for him in his room since she had a key. Charlotte was aggravated by the fact that Laverne had access to Jake's room, and she couldn't get in. Surprisingly, Roxie also had a problem with Jake having a girlfriend. She was starting to feel like the new, distinguished, and vibrant young lady was dimming the spotlight that Jake had always seen her in.

Charlotte started doing little things to agitate Laverne. When Laverne walked inside the house, Charlotte would call her something else, as if she was mistaking her for another one of Jakes's girlfriends. Sometimes, she would tell Laverne that Jake had another woman over the night before. Laverne was good at ignoring Charlotte which made her angrier. Laverne was not a fighter. Charlotte wasn't either, but she knew Laverne was afraid of her. One day, Laverne came over to wait on Jake after work, and Charlotte blocked the hallway to keep her from getting through. Laverne said, "Excuse me," with her head down, looking at the floor. Charlotte shoved her to the floor and started hitting and kicking her, but because of her habit, she soon became winded. Laverne fought back enough to get away and lock herself in Jake's room. When Jake got home, he found Laverne sitting on his bed crying, her shirt was torn, and her hair was disarrayed. He knew something bad had happened and it was all the doings of Charlotte. Laverne explained what had happened and Jake charged out of the room to tell Charlotte she had to get out. Roxie was just walking in the door with groceries. Charlotte went and got a metal baseball bat that she kept in her apartment when she lived alone in the city. When she tried to hit Jake with the bat, he shoved her so hard, she fell and hit her head on the center table in the living room. Roxie called 911. When the police arrived, Jake was taken into custody. Ralph came home shortly afterward. When Roxie told him what had happened, he drove down to the police department and posted bail for Jake. After Jake was released, he stayed at a lodge until his court date.

When Jake went to court, to his dismay, Roxie was sitting on the bench beside Charlotte. Jake could not believe what he was seeing. News traveled fast in Meadow Brook. A lot of people in the town spoke well of Jake, how they never knew him to get into any trouble, how he was honest and hardworking. As for Charlotte, her reputation was nowhere near as polished. Jake's eyes began to fill with water, not because he feared what the judge was about to say. He was thinking about how much he had done for Roxie, taking care of her when she was ill and making sure she had food to eat and the bills were paid. When her car broke down, he bought her another one. Jake was starting to feel bitterness like he had never felt before, the same kind that his grandfather told him a woman can make a man feel when he was a young boy. Jake knew he could not live under the same roof as Charlotte and Roxie anymore. At this point, he didn't care what happened with the house. "What's next?" he thought to himself. Jake took a deep breath, continuing to look straight and focusing on the judge. Fortunately, Jake found favor with Judge Taylor. After both sides were heard, Jake was released with no jail time or probation, but he was warned that he probably needed to change his living arrangements. The situation about Jacob and why James left was never properly explained to Jake, he just knew that a new child showed up and his father chose him over his family. Feeling abandoned by his father for an outside child, and now, Roxie choosing Charlotte over him, Jake's distrust, and lack of respect for women had reached its peak.

When Jake left the courtroom, he stayed at the lodge for a few more days, then he went to his house to gather more of his belongings. Jake had purchased a couple of acres further west for hunting which he didn't tell Roxie about. Jake's grandfather told him to never tell a woman how much money he had or tell her everything he was doing. Now, he was thinking about building a new house on that property. Jake had to move in with his grandparents for about a year until he got situated and could start building his house. It was uncomfortable, but Jake didn't believe in wasting any more money than he had to, the hardest part was going from living under his own roof - to living under somebody else's, even if it was temporary. This would also be the first time he encountered his father in years.

Jake worked 12-hour shifts every day. One morning, he went outside to warm his truck and realized he forgot to fill up his tank the night before. Jake hadn't been to the bank either, so he didn't have any cash. His grandfather had a gas jug and a funnel behind the house, Jake just needed to walk to the gas station to get some gas. He knew his father didn't have much money, he was disabled, and drank most of his income. Jake was very independent so it took all the strength he had to humble himself and ask James if he had five bucks he could borrow until he went to the bank Saturday morning. Jake didn't remember asking his father for anything as a child. According to Roxie, his father never did anything for him either, so Jake thought his father would be glad to lend him the money. James reached into his pocket, pulled out a few dollars and said, "Here, and make sure you pay me back," Jake looked at him as if to say, "Are you serious…you never did anything for me." Jake didn't have time to discuss it, he took the money, went and got the gas, and left for work. Jake paid his father back Saturday morning and never asked him for another dime.

# 23

## ROXIE'S PASSING

Jake finally met with another contractor and they came up with a floor plan, exactly the way he wanted his new home built. It wouldn't be long before his house was completed, and he would be able to move out of his grandparent's house. This would be Jake's first home without Roxie. He returned to the first house he built with Roxie one more time, to gather the remainder of his things. When Jake entered the house, the energy had changed so much. It didn't feel like the same house he had built. Roxie was in her bedroom, but she knew it was him. He had a distinctive sound apart from Ralph when he opened the door and walked through the house. Perhaps, it was because he was much taller, stockier, and he took heavier steps when he walked. When Jake passed by Roxie's room, she was sitting on her bed. She caught a sad glimpse of him as he passed by, but she never mumbled a word, just as she did when James left. Jake went downstairs to the garage and got all his outdoor equipment, and that was the last time Roxie would get that close to Jake for many years. Jake was still friends with Roxie's neighbors, and he would visit them from time to time. Roxie would see him standing outside near the yard, but he never came her way and she never bothered to speak to him either.

After Jake left, Roxie's health started declining until she was unable to work anymore. Ralph moved out and Charlotte had become more of a burden than a helper. The biggest choice Roxie faced every month was paying for her medication or the mortgage and the utilities. Roxie was sitting on the edge of her bed one afternoon, and she heard a conversation in the living room. She mustered up the strength to get out of bed and see who it was. When she got to the living room, it was Charlotte, laughing and giggling with one of Roxie's old acquaintances. Roxie was upset about what she saw, and she had some harsh words to say to Charlotte and Jimmy. Jimmy got up and left. On the way back to her room, Roxie noticed the pile of mail on the living room table. There was a "Notice Envelope." When Roxie opened it, the mortgage was three months in default. Roxie had been sending Charlotte to mail the mortgage payment but apparently, she had not been doing so. Roxie got into a big argument with Charlotte, and she moved out with a friend shortly thereafter. Roxie was left alone living in the house that Jake built for her.

One day Ralph stopped by to check on Roxie, he was distraught to see the deplorable living condition she was in. There was no heat, water, or food in the house. Ralph had to work every day and Roxie needed a full-time caregiver. He had no choice but to put her in a nursing home. Ralph would visit her, but Charlotte nor Jake ever came to see her. One day, Ralph got a phone call regarding Roxie's continued declining health, she had been moved to the hospital and he was told to call all the family in.

When Jake wasn't working, he was always in the woods, he had become a true outdoorsman. Ralph could not get him on the phone, so he drove over to his house. When Jake returned home, he saw Ralph sitting in his yard, he thought he was coming to visit. As Jake was unloading his hunting equipment, Ralph walked over and told him that if he ever wanted to see his mother alive again, he needed to get to the hospital immediately. Jake didn't know what to think. His bitterness and unforgiveness had clouded his perception of the elapsed time, assuming his mother would be around forever. Jake thought he was simply punishing

Roxie by having nothing to do with her, but his distant grudge was killing her slowly.

Jake went to see Roxie at the hospital, but he stayed at a distance, never getting close enough to express any emotion. Roxie was aware that he was there, but she had no strength left to speak. Shortly afterward, she took her last breath. Ralph called Jake outside and told him that Roxie had a small life insurance policy from her previous employer, but not enough to pay for the entire funeral expenses. Whatever she had left in her savings account, Charlotte must have cleaned it out. Jake jumped to the task, no questions asked. He picked out Roxie's dress, jewelry, shoes, and casket. Jake even requested that her hair was pressed and curled the way he remembered it when he was a child. She may have lived her last days in undesirable conditions, but Jake was determined that her departure would be that of Royalty.

During the funeral service, Charlotte really put on a show. That was the first time Jake had seen her in over 10 years. As she started walking towards the casket, her legs became limp and the ushers had to brace her. When she gathered herself enough to approach the casket, she placed her hand on the side of it and fainted, almost pulling the entire casket off the stand. Jake had thoughts of picking her up, throwing her in the casket with Roxie and locking it, since she was pretending to be so attached. Jake requested to have Roxie carried to the cemetery by horses in a glass carriage through town after the service. At the burial site, Jake was front and center. After Roxie was committed back to the ground, Jake stepped off to the side. Leading up to this very moment, his adrenaline had been fueled by the idea that Roxie still needed him, even in death. Jake believed she could see everything he was doing for her, but he knew the shovels and the mound of dirt represented the end was near, and he had to face his biggest emotional giant. The woman who praised him for everything he did and acknowledged him as being a man when he was just a boy, was gone forever. As Jake stood there with his hands in his pockets, a stranger appeared from out of nowhere, instantaneously startling him. The stranger had a slight stagger, Jake thought to himself, who comes to a funeral drunk, not to mention lingering beside a six-foot hole in the ground. The stranger looked at Jake, he had piercing eyes that looked to hold ancient wisdom and the secrets to eternity. He was short, with a slight hump in his back, and his clothes appeared to be from a different time. Speaking soft and slow, he said, "Anger is a very strong force, you can neither control it nor contain it, but you must release it. If you do not, it will come out when you least expect it, causing great harm. Whenever you have unfinished business in your heart with a person who is no longer on this side, find a quiet place, and invite the soul of the individual to join you. Tell them how you feel and release their soul. You can even ask for forgiveness if you need too." Jake looked down at the ground while deep in his thoughts. The same way the stranger appeared, he vanished instantly. Jake looked around to see where he went, but he was nowhere in sight. Jake pondered on the words of the stranger, then his pride forced him to toss the idea into the wind, just in case anyone else heard the conversation and would agree that he was wrong for not forgiving his own mother while she was living. Jake felt he was the one who was entitled to an apology.

Everybody complimented Ralph on how well their mother looked, then out of nowhere, came Charlotte. She was dressed more for a night on the town, than her mother's funeral. She wreaked of alcohol, as she said to Ralph, "Now that momma is dead, who is really Jake's father?" Ralph looked at her and said, "Charlotte...Really? Really?" "I was just asking. "You know he has never looked like any of us." Ralph stood there ignoring her, hoping his silence would drive her away. He knew his mother didn't have the best reputation, in fact, he took part in orchestrating some of her infidelities. Ralph felt his mother's name had been dragged through the dirt enough, but today was the day that her life would be honored and celebrated.

# 24

## MATT STARTS A NEW LIFE

Matt was enrolled in St. Mary's School of Seminary and he was working hard towards his Theology degree.

One day, while working on a construction job near Bill's Place, a young lady with light skin and reddish-brown hair was carrying boxes of beverages up the ramp and into the side door. Matt stopped for a minute - to wipe the sweat from his brow. He wasn't the kind of guy that was easily distracted, but Phoebe was beautiful, she was Bill's daughter, the owner of the bar. It was break time anyway, and Matt and his Uncle Phil were about to go across the street and grab a burger. Phoebe smiled at Matt and he smiled back at her. Being a man of the cloth, he never thought he would meet a woman at a bar, but Phoebe was different. She looked as if she was part of the business, it wasn't like she was sitting around drinking, smoking, or mingling with the guys.

At Bob's Burger Joint, Matt sat with his uncle and the rest of the crew. "I saw Bill's daughter checking you out and you weren't shy about noticing her either. You should ask her out." Matt smiled but Phil knew what he was thinking, so he said, "Marie will be all right, it's time for you to follow your own heart." Matt thought about what his uncle said and finished eating his burger while gazing across the street - hoping he could get another glimpse of Phoebe. Matt returned to the construction site and worked until the end of his shift, but Phoebe never came back outside.

When he got home, he took a shower and went into the kitchen to see what Marie had prepared for dinner. Marie noticed that Matt was quiet at the table, but she didn't say anything. He was thinking about Phoebe and his graduation.

Several days passed at the construction site, and Matt saw no sign of the beautiful woman, who had captured his attention earlier during the week. It was lunchtime, and instead of going across the street to get a burger, Matt had brought his lunch from home. He let the tailgate down on the back of Phil's crew cab and sat there, eating his ham sandwich, and drinking his sweet tea. There she was, just appearing out of nowhere, wearing a white ruffled blouse and a blue skirt with navy blue pumps. This time, she walked over towards Matt. "Hi, my name is Phoebe," she said, with her hand stretched out in Matt's direction. Matt was kind of embarrassed, he didn't want Phoebe to feel his hard, calloused hands from shoveling, but he didn't want to be rude either. "If only she could have seen him in his Sunday attire with his hands moisturized," he thought. Matt shook Phoebe's hand and told her his name. "That's my father's bar over there." "I kind of figured that," said Matt, in a courteous tone with a slight smile. "You didn't go to Meadow Brook High, did you?" he asked. "No," Phoebe replied, "I grew up in Greenville with my mother, but I majored in business at college. I came back here to help my father manage the bar." "That's why I didn't recognize you," said Matt. "I'm about to graduate Seminary School," he said. "Oh, a man of the cloth," she replied. That didn't turn Phoebe off, she had a good feeling about Matt. They talked for a little while then Phoebe left, and Matt went back to work.

Phoebe and Matt started dating shortly thereafter, and he brought her home to meet Marie. The biggest hurdle that he faced would be telling Marie that he was getting ready to move on. Matt graduated from Seminary School and became the Assistant Pastor of Meadow Brook Holiness/Pentecostal Church. It would not be long before he would be ready to ask Phoebe's father for her hand in marriage. Marie knew the day was coming, that Matt would find someone and start a family of his own, but she was not expecting it to happen so abruptly. Dinner was bittersweet and Marie was very quiet.

Matt and Phoebe got married at the church with a simple, sweet, ceremony and reception. Looking ahead, Matt knew that the construction job was not dependable enough to provide for a family. During rainy seasons, he could miss weeks of work at a time, so he applied for a job at the Vintage Oats, Cereal Company. Matt moved up to management before long, and he only worked construction if his uncle needed an extra hand on the weekends. A year later, Matt and Phoebe had a baby girl named Jacqueline and two years later, another daughter named Patricia. They decided that it would be best for Phoebe to stay home with the girls and keep the house, instead of running the bar. Phoebe was not a good cook, but Matt was, he had gotten plenty of practice by cooking for his brothers and sisters when his mother was working or at night school. Jacqueline and Patricia grew to become very responsible girls - just like their father. Matt and the girls would dress up and he would take them out on dinner dates to give Phoebe a break and show them how a gentleman should treat them when it's time for them to start dating. When the girls were in middle school, Matt and Phoebe were surprised by another pregnancy. Matt could not have been more proud to have a son. They named him John. All the memories of Matt's childhood came flooding back to his mind while he was standing there in the delivery room holding John. Matt loved that little boy with all his heart, and he knew he would never abandon him. Matt would do anything in the world for his son, and there was so much he wanted to teach him about becoming a man. As John grew older, Matt never neglected the opportunity to play catch with him. He signed John up for every sport he wanted to play, and Matt never missed a game.

One Sunday, Matt arrived at church and his pastor; Reverend Wells announced that he wanted to meet with all the members after church. He had already met with the trustees and the decision board one day during the week. They wanted to give him the opportunity to speak to the congregation in his own words. Rev. Wells was getting older and he didn't have the energy or the memory that he once had. He felt that it was getting time for him to retire.

Matt thought Reverend Wells should have retired years ago, but he wasn't going to be the one to say it. Rev. Wells suggested that Matt would make a great replacement for him. He wanted the congregation to think about it over the next week and come back with their decisions. Rev. Wells had been faithful to the congregation, but everybody knew it was time for him to pass the torch to a younger, more youthful spirited minister.

The following Sunday, Matt would be voted the pastor of Meadow Brook Holiness/Pentecostal Church. His installation service was scheduled two weeks later. Now that Matt would become the full-time pastor and receive a wage, he could quit the part-time construction job. After Matt's installation as Senior Pastor- Phoebe, Jacqueline, and Patricia would help clean the church on Saturdays. John usually played football on the weekends or hung out with his friends. The prophecy over Matt's life would prove to be true in just a matter of time. Matt's gift of prophecy, teaching, and counseling skills drew a lot of people to the church. Within five years, the church was flourishing and overflowing to the point that they had to make the decision to build a new church beside the old one. The old facility was turned into a food bank for the less fortunate in the community. Matt's family no longer had to maintain the old building. The church could afford to hire janitors, so Matt could spend more time being a pastor.

As the congregation continued to grow over the years, the Trustee Board offered Matt a generous wage and all the members approved it. Matt's income from the church enabled him to quit working at the Vintage Oats, Cereal Company and pastor full time.

Jacqueline and Patricia didn't mind sharing clothes, they had always shared everything, but John always wore the latest fashions, and since he was the only boy, he never had to share anything with his older sisters. Matt did everything he could to keep John from having the same childhood that he had. John was very popular in school and with the kids at church, but unlike his father, he was very rude and inconsiderate. While his father prayed for the less fortunate parents and children in the church, John made fun of them. Most kids who were not in John's clique, tried to avoid him altogether, even the older kids and Matt never noticed his behavior. There was a young guy named Donald at the church, who was socially awkward, but a genius in Math and Science. He was about 5 years older than John. Donald's parents bought his clothes from second-hand stores and his shoes from Dollar Plus. Donald's clothes never fit right, they were either too big, too short or too tight. One day, Donald was in the Board Room, reading a book while waiting for his parents to come out of a Leadership meeting in the Conference Room. John and his cool friends came in and sat down. Donald knew it wouldn't be long before they started making fun of him, so he got up to leave. As much as he dreaded to do so, Donald had to pass by John and his friends. They all got quiet when Donald walked by, then suddenly, John stuck his foot out, tripping Donald. Donald fell and knocked over five chairs - almost landing on his glasses. John and his friends laughed so loud. Donald got up and dusted himself off. He placed his glasses back on his face, straightened the chairs back up, and walked away without saying a word.

As John grew older, Matt started to notice that he was very rebellious, he couldn't get him to do anything around the house and he didn't study hard to get good grades like Matt did when he was in school. John couldn't do half the things that Matt was able to do when he was his age. Matt's daughters had gone off to college and were doing well for themselves. It was becoming very common for Matt to lose his temper at John. The children in the congregation reverenced Matt more than his own son did. The years had slipped by so fast. Matt didn't even know if John had intentions of going to college. Scarred by his mother's reputation as a child, Matt's biggest fear was that John was not going to do anything with his life or might end up getting into trouble and making him look bad as a pastor.

# 25

## JAKE RESURFACES

Now that the funeral was over, Jake still had not gotten over what happened between himself, Roxie, and Charlotte and those frustrations would be taken out on anyone caught in his path. Jake had always been very opinionated, but now, it was worse. He was starting to realize that his good deeds for Roxie's burial did not heal his broken heart. Jake's suppressed emotions began to incubate a rage that was bigger than himself. When Roxie was living, Jake didn't care to go around anybody that had anything to do with her or Charlotte. Jake was a good guy, but when you crossed him, it was over. He was stubborn like Roxie, but he also had a lot of ways like his grandfather. All of Jake's relatives agreed that what happened to him was unfair, but over time, everyone had moved on and encouraged him to do the same, but he chose to distance himself from everybody.

At Roxie's repass, Jake saw relatives that he had not seen in years and he realized, whether he chose to distance himself or not, his family and friends kept moving forward. They had not changed, and they were still glad to see him as they were - the day that he chose to step away from everybody. Jake enjoyed talking to his family and he realized that people aren't meant to be alone, neither should they spend more time with nature than one another.

Jake liked the way everybody marveled at Roxie's nice going-away ceremony, but he knew the praises would soon dwindle. Jake decided to purchase an expensive sports car - to show everybody that despite the misfortune of losing his first house, he was still doing well. Nobody could believe it. They knew he had a lot of money because he worked hard and saved all the time, but he was very stingy, and he was only known to spend large amounts of money on Roxie. Jake started making surprise visits to different relative's houses. At first, everybody was glad to see him, and his appearance made people think he was finally moving on, until about five minutes into the conversation. He usually started by asking how everybody was doing and then, out of nowhere, he would throw a fireball question that was complicated or controversial, which would insult somebody's job, favorite political party, or diet. Jake would go on and on about how much money he had in the bank. If he knew somebody in his family was a Christian, he would go on a rant about how Christianity was the darkest, bloodiest religion in history. He never had anything positive to say, and he always had to be right. Whatever anybody was cooking when he stopped by their house, they had to start from the beginning, listing all the ingredients they used and telling him every step they took, so that he could tell them everything they did wrong, even if it was as simple as boiling water for spaghetti. "Did you boil the water too high, too low, too long or not long enough? What did you season it with?" he would ask. If you didn't own as many guns, knives, or hunting bows as he did, you weren't a man.

It wasn't long before Jake started to take his frustrations out on Laverne. He started to find every little thing to complain about. She hardly ever cooked or kept the house tidy, but Laverne felt that she shouldn't have to because they both had jobs outside the home. When Jake cooked, she appreciated him but never praised him the way Roxie did after her surgery. Jake started complaining about Laverne's outer appearance. Certainly, she had gained some weight since high school, but not enough to cause a health scare or to consider ending the relationship.

Laverne was very independent, as she was a Corporate Accountant and she made more money than Jake. She didn't need Jake to take care of her and even though she was nice, she had better things to do other than praise Jake all day. Unlike Roxie, Laverne never validated Jake as a man, as far as she was concerned, he should already know whether he was a man or not.

Jake fell out of favor with his hunting buddies, since their wives didn't fit into his standard of beauty either, it was just too uncomfortable having him around. Jake's friends were Laverne's friends, and they loved her nice personality, but they were put in uncomfortable predicaments when Jake would talk about other women in front of her.

When anybody asked how his sister was doing, he would make jokes about choking her if she ever got close to him again. His stories became so chauvinistic and violent that nobody wanted to be around him anymore.

It was obvious that Jake's anger had manifested into a beast over the years. Before long, everybody was talking about Jake and avoiding him as much as possible. Nobody answered their phones anymore when he called, and they would pretend they weren't home when he showed up.

# 26

## CAREER CHANGE

Jake decided that he was tired of working for Wade Concrete and he wanted to try his hands at something different. He was able to get a job out of the elements and into the automotive industry. Unlike his previous-all men's crew, Jake's new job allowed him to work with lots of women, and they certainly had eyes for him, especially one lady named Raquel Rodriguez. Her mother was Honduran, and her father was African American but they never married. She worked on an assembly line - packaging oxygen sensors. Jake had to pull parts for her department and place them on a pallet near her line with his forklift. Every time Jake dropped off a pallet of parts in Raquel's department, she would get her clipboard from the desk to have Jake sign off on the delivery and he would start flirting with her.

One day, Jake was sitting in the break room and Raquel walked in. All the tables were filled, but there was one seat left in front of Jake. When Raquel finished heating her lunch in the microwave, she asked Jake if anyone was sitting in front of him and he kindly replied, "No." Raquel sat on the bench and placed a steaming mixture of beef on the table while she unwrapped her heated tortillas, shredded cabbage, and homemade spicy salsa. "Would you like some?" she asked. "What is it?" asked Jake. Raquel didn't bother to explain, she was so confident in her cooking skills that she just rolled up a tortilla stuffed with everything she had and told Jake to taste it. Jake thought to himself, "Laverne never cook like this, in fact, she doesn't cook at all." Raquel told Jake, back home in Honduras, her mother gets up before the sun rises to make homemade tortillas and she taught her the same. Their conversation was something Jake had never talked about in his life, but it seemed as if the conversation ended as soon as it started. Before he knew it, Raquel was whipping her long wavy hair over her shoulder and packing up her stuff saying, "Break is almost over." Jake didn't hear a word she said, he was so mesmerized by her beauty, then he heard the buzzer go off and he realized that he was supposed to be on his forklift already.

The next day Jake came to work, he was looking forward to seeing Raquel. He went to deliver parts to her assembly line, but she wasn't there. He sat in the break room at the same table on the same chair, but Raquel didn't show up. Another forklift driver named Rick, saw how Jake stayed focused on the door waiting for Raquel to walk in, so he came over and said, "Hey man, I saw you talking to Raquel yesterday." Jake just looked at him as if to say, "What about it?" "Well, you seem like a pretty nice guy. I just want to warn you, Raquel is a very attractive woman, but most of the guys in the warehouse have dated her at one time or another. I wouldn't go down that road if I were you. Let's just say...she doesn't have the best reputation around here, neither does she have a squeaky-clean record, if you know what I mean." Jake listened but he didn't know whether to trust Rick, after all, he could just be jealous.

During the drive home, Jake pondered on everything Rick had said. The next day when he went to drop the parts off in Raquel's department, she appeared to be very busy, so she sent another worker from the line to take the clipboard over for Jake to sign off on it. Raquel spent her entire break on the phone and Jake didn't get a chance to talk to her. Little did Jake know; Raquel had a boyfriend. She had missed work the day before because he had been released from prison, and she had to pick him up. Raquel's boyfriend was a career criminal. He wouldn't be out long before he would do something else, stealing, armed robbery, carjacking, you name it, and sometimes, he would drag Raquel into his twisted schemes. If Raquel had a choice, she wouldn't be with Juan, but she was afraid of him because he was crazy.

An entire week had passed before Raquel came and sat with Jake in the break room again. Jake's first response was, *"Long time no see, stranger."* Juan had been home for a week, and Raquel was getting tired of him already. Juan refused to get a job, he drank beer all day, ate all the groceries, and complained about what she didn't have. Seeing Jake was like a breath of fresh air. Over time, Jake and Raquel became more and more friendly towards each other. Even though Jake could see Rick shaking his head at him from a distance sometimes in the break room, he continued to talk to Raquel.

Jake had started talking to Raquel on the phone at night, not caring whether Lavern heard him or not. Laverne was very passive and easy-going, but for the first time in seven years, she was starting to wonder if her relationship with Jake was really in jeopardy.

Juan was asleep in the back room one night while Raquel was talking to Jake on the phone. Raquel's giggling woke him up. Juan got out of the bed and started walking slowly towards the room that he heard the sound coming from. Suddenly, Raquel felt her head being snatched backward by her long wavy hair. "Who are you talking to?" asked Juan, "Laughing out loud like that!" Raquel hung up the phone immediately and said, "No one, it was just a friend." Juan pulled Raquel out of the chair by her hair and he snatched the phone cord out of the jack in the wall. Jake didn't know what had happened. He tried to call back, but there was no answer and that was probably a good thing, at least for Raquel.

When Jake saw Raquel at work the next day, she had a busted lip and a black eye. During break, he asked her what happened, and she said, "When I was laughing last night on the phone, I accidentally fell out of the chair and hit my face on the corner of the coffee table." Jake had a strange look on his face, but he didn't question it. "I was wondering if you would like to come to my place and watch a movie?" he asked. Raquel responded hesitantly, I.... don't know, it would have to be immediately after work. Jake knew Lavern would be going over to her sister's house after work, the same sister who had been telling her she should leave him. He and Laverne weren't really speaking anyway, other than his harsh insults. Laverne was good at dodging Jake's fiery darts and that aggravated him. It just fueled his arrogance.

By the end of the workday, Raquel had agreed to go to Jake's house for a little while. They talked and got to know each other better. When Lavern pulled into the driveway later that afternoon, she saw Raquel backing out. She didn't get a good look at the driver, but she knew it was a woman. When she came inside the house, she asked Jake who was the woman pulling out of the driveway. In a childish kind of way, he liked that Laverne was jealous, this meant he had her full attention. Jake didn't respond, he just got up and went to get a shower.

Friday afternoon, when Jake got home from work, Laverne was getting ready for a night out with some of her co-workers. Jake was in the garage working out, and she told him that she would see him later. When Laverne returned home that night, it felt different in the house as soon as she opened the door and turned the light on. The house was spotless, something she did not take pride in, and there was a fragrance in the air that didn't smell like any of her perfumes. Raquel had been there earlier. Jake was doing things to intentionally agitate Laverne while failing to address the greater emptiness that needed filling.

When Raquel got back to her trailer, she opened the front door and went inside, Juan was standing behind the door when she closed it. As soon as she noticed him, she dropped her keys, lunch box, and pocketbook on the floor. "Juan!" she gasped while grabbing her chest, "You scared me." "Where have you been?" he demanded, after pulling the beer can down from his mouth and swallowing. "Nowhere," Raquel responded. Juan slammed the palm of his hand on the kitchen table and Raquel ran to the bedroom and locked the door. Juan trashed the trailer and fell asleep. Raquel got up the next morning, got dressed, and creeped out of the door to go to work.

When Juan woke up, he stumbled down the hall, wiping the crust out of his eyes and looking for Raquel. Juan walked two trailers over to his buddy's house and told him he thinks Raquel is seeing someone else. "Who do you think it is?" Antonio asked. "I don't know, it could be somebody she works with," said Juan. Antonio agreed to give Juan a ride to Raquel's job. They showed up around the normal time that she would be clocking out and parked at the end of the lot where Raquel couldn't see them. Shortly after 3:30 in the afternoon, Raquel came stepping outside the warehouse with Jake behind her. "I knew it," said Juan. Jake walked Raquel over to her car and lowered his head to the window to say goodbye. Juan was furious. Raquel went home, but Antonio and Juan followed Jake, to see where he lived.

# 27

## CIVILIAN LIFE

After being discharged from the military, I settled in Birmingham in a small studio apartment. I wrote to Uncle Daniel to let him know where I was and that I was all right. He wrote back and asked me to come visit. I thought to myself, what could it hurt? I could at least see how Ron and Cindy were doing.

When I arrived in Meadow Brook on Sunday afternoon, the neighborhood looked pretty much the same. There it was, the building I had come to know throughout my childhood, which had so many bad memories and had catapulted me on the journey I am on today. I did not know if I should knock or just open the door and walk inside. I had not anticipated so many dreaded memories flooding back while standing outside that door. As I got ready to knock on the door, Uncle Daniel opened it. He had a bag of trash that he was taking to the dumpsters behind the apartment buildings. When he saw me, he dropped the bag immediately and gave me a hug, I thought he was going to squeeze the breath out of me. He had tears in his eyes as he was patting me on the back. "You gained some weight and some muscle in the military huh?" "Yeah," I replied. Lena came out of the kitchen, where she was still preparing Sunday dinner for the parishioners from church. Momma was oddly quiet though. I didn't know if I should speak to her or not. Uncle Daniel told me that she had a stroke shortly after I left and had not fully recovered. Lena stared at me as though she was lost for words, then she walked over slowly and gave me a hug. I don't know if she did it because it was the appropriate thing for her to do in front of the guests, but it made me feel awkward.

I spoke to everyone sitting at the table, then I went to the restroom to wash my hands. When I went back to the kitchen to fix my plate, I felt like I was doing something illegal, by eating at the same time as the parishioners. I grabbed a chair and sat off to the side since there was no more room at the table. I asked Uncle Daniel where Ron and Cindy were. He said Cindy was downstairs at Mandy's apartment, her friend from school. Then he paused and said, "I tried to get Ron to do something like you or go to college, but I think your momma spoiled that boy. He started hanging with those guys from the pool hall and got himself in some serious trouble." "What kind of trouble?" I asked. "Well, they got busted for selling hot car parts. We just went to visit him the other day and he should be home in a couple of months." As Uncle Daniel kept talking, I happened to notice that Deacon Whitaker kept smiling at Lena and when he raised his cup to ask if she would bring him some more tea, I saw something that looked very familiar but I could not make out where I had seen it before. That black sapphire, where have I seen it…," I kept thinking to myself. Then it hit me like a ton of bricks… that was my father's ring. I didn't want to eat another bite, I felt as if my food was about to become regurgitated. I did not want to spend another minute in that apartment. I told Uncle Daniel I should be getting back on the road before it gets too late. He walked with me outside because he wanted to talk a little while longer, but I could not focus on anything he was saying. On the way home, all I could think about was that ring.

I had applied for several jobs when I was released from the military. About three weeks later, I got a call from Carter's Printing Factory. The job was easy, it didn't take long to learn how to operate the printing press. By the end of the week, I was reaching the production level. There was a young lady named Glenda who worked another press across from me, and we would meet up where the ink jugs were stationed to get refills. We were total opposites, but somehow, that drew us together, or either I just overlooked a lot of things because I was blindsided by her beauty, charm, quick wit and the fact that she could cook better than Lena. We started hanging out together after work. After dating for about a year, we decided to get married. The ceremony was nothing special, just a trip to the courthouse. I didn't invite any of my family, I was almost afraid for Glenda to meet them. I knew my family was dysfunctional, but I never realized the severity of it until I was faced with having to introduce someone to them. Glenda decided not to invite her family either.

On Saturday mornings, I would go for a run just like I did in the military. At the beginning of our relationship, Glenda would run with me, but shortly thereafter, she stopped, her cigarette habit caused her to struggle with her breathing. Glenda's smoking agitated me more after we were married than when we were dating. She also had a serious gambling problem that surfaced, and she would travel great distances to casinos with her friends. What was worse, she couldn't keep a job. Shortly after we got married, she quit working at the Printing Factory.

I had a few struggles too, especially one that I hoped Glenda would never find out about. I was curious about girls at a very young age and I struggled to keep pure thoughts when talking to them, as far back as I could remember. I had not dated many girls because I also struggled with intimacy. Whenever I tried to be intimate with Glenda, she wanted the lights off and I had to have the lights on, otherwise, my flow would always come to a halt. I couldn't keep a certain image out of my head that taunted me since childhood. If the lights were off, my imagination tormented me to believe that I was touching the body of someone else other than Glenda.

One day, out of the nowhere, I received a letter from Lena, she said she needed some money. I felt intimidated to send it right away, I didn't even ask what it was for. My immediate response set the tone for how I would furnish everything that she and Ron would need in the future. I didn't tell Glenda, but I wired $300 to Lena. Even though we did not communicate regularly, I felt that this was one way of proving to Lena that I was a better man than my father. I was responsible, and I had money saved for emergencies, even though Glenda and I were just starting out and we had a few financial struggles.

Glenda and I had been married for two years now. We were watching a movie when the phone rang. It was Lena. She still spoke to me in an angry and hostile tone, just like she did before I left home. I was embarrassed and I didn't want Glenda to hear her yelling through the phone. Glenda got up to go to the kitchen and asked if I wanted something to drink. Lena wanted to know who was talking to me in the background. I didn't dare tell her I had gotten married, she insulted everything I ever did and every decision I ever made. When Glenda walked away, I told Lena it was my girlfriend. She bombarded me with a plethora of questions, where did you meet her at? Does she have a job or is she just after your money? My responses were very soft as I didn't want to alarm Glenda. "Well, I called because your brother is having a hard time finding a job and he needs to borrow some money." Even though it bothered me to give over my hard- earned money, especially not knowing if I would ever see it again, I asked how much he needed. I wired Ron $500 and I didn't hear from him or Lena for a while.

A year later, Lena called and said, "I'm coming to your house, so tell me how to get there!" I was so lost for words. I could barely swallow, but I should have known that day was coming, eventually. I had already met

Glenda's family. I don't know why I thought she would never meet mine. Glenda came from a large family and she was the youngest, so her parents were elderly and kind. The reason why I moved so far away from Meadow Brook was because I was trying to reinvent myself and start over. I didn't tell Glenda, they were coming, I just hoped that if there was such a thing as miracles, they would change their mind. Besides, I couldn't figure out why Lena wanted to visit me, she hated me as a child and Ron was always her favorite.

Late Saturday morning around 11:00, there was a knock at the door, I was washing dishes. When I get nervous, I start fidgeting around the house. Glenda was doing the crossword puzzle in the newspaper. She put her cigarette out and laid the newspaper down and answered the door. When she opened the door, there stood Lena, Momma, and Ron. Cindy had gone to the mall with her friends. Glenda didn't know what to say. When I came from the kitchen, I could see Lena staring at Glenda as if her eyes were peering through her soul. I tried to break the tension by asking everybody to come in and have a seat. I asked how everybody was doing, but I noticed Glenda felt out of place with all these people showing up unexpected, whom I had never mentioned. Somehow, I got around having to introduce them to Glenda, nobody was interested in getting to know her. Ron started telling crazy stories to get everybody in a good mood, only for me to let down my guard so that he could suggest that we go outside and have a talk. When we walked outside onto the back porch, he told me that he had moved out and he was trying to make it on his own, but he keeps coming up short. He asked if he could hold a couple of dollars until he got paid. At that time, Glenda and I were sharing a car and I told him that I was saving up for a new one since the transmission in my other car had torn up. I felt like it would be better to just buy another car. I had a hard time saying no to my family. "Let me see what I can do," I told him, and we walked back inside the house.

By that time, Lena came over to me and said she needed to go to the store. We got in the car, leaving Glenda at home, feeling out of place with Ron and Momma. On the way to the store, Lena asked if I had the money to help Ron. I told her I really don't, because I needed a new car, and he never paid me what he already owed me. "What do you mean... what he already owes you?" she shouted. "That's your brother and family take care of family! If you got it, you need to let him have it! I see you taking care of that woman! Sitting down here on all that money and don't want to let anybody have any of it!" "What money?" I replied. "I'm just trying to make it like everybody else, but I can't... if I got to keep taking care of a grown man." When we arrived at the grocery store, Lena grabbed a grocery cart and I couldn't figure out why. She got squash, sweet potatoes, cauliflower, beef brisket, chicken wings, and potatoes. We basically went grocery shopping for a month. When we got to the register, all the items rang up to over $200. Lena went to reach in her purse, but I couldn't let her do that, so I just pulled out my credit card and paid for the groceries. Lena didn't say a word, she just smiled at me and then the cashier, as if to say, "I trained him well."

When we got back to the house, I carried the groceries inside. Glenda was sitting there looking confused. Ron was watching TV and Momma was quiet, she still had not recovered completely from the stroke. Glenda asked, "Why do you have all those groceries, Timothy?" I didn't know what to say, so I didn't say anything. I was too scared to make Lena upset in front of Glenda for fear that she would start shouting and hitting me like she did before I left home. Lena went into the kitchen and started rumbling through Glenda's pots and pans and started prepping the food. "What is she doing?" Glenda asked. I acted as if I didn't hear her, then Glenda got up and went to our bedroom and shut the door. I wanted to check on her, but I did not want Lena to think Glenda had gotten upset with her, so I didn't bother. When the food was done, I went to turn the doorknob to our bedroom, but it was locked. I asked Glenda if she wanted something to eat, but she didn't answer... so I went back to the kitchen. I told everybody that she wasn't feeling well, so we all sat down at the table and ate without her.

After everybody left, Glenda and I did not speak for a week. Our non-communication might have been a good thing because we had planned to pick out a used car this month, but I didn't know how to tell her that I had given Ron the money. Six months later, I had the money to pay down on the car that I wanted, just in time for the winter, so I wouldn't have to freeze at the bus stops when Glenda was using our only car.

It was the middle of winter and snow was predicted to come through Northern Alabama. The night before it snowed, Ron showed up. He had caught a bus to my house, he didn't need money this time, he needed transportation. I talked to Glenda about letting Ron borrow the older car. Glenda didn't like Ron from the first time she met him. She summed him up as an over aged, irresponsible kid, and she didn't care to see Lena again either. Glenda didn't want to let him borrow the car, but I let him have it anyway. It snowed Tuesday. Lena called Thursday to tell me that Ron was driving in the snow and lost control of the car. He slid into an embankment and didn't know how to tell me. He just left the car beside the road. I asked her where he had left it, so I could have it towed. A week later, the insurance company totaled the car. This brought a rift between me and Glenda, but it wouldn't be the last of Ron showing up to borrow things that he had no intention of returning.

Over the years, Lena started showing up unannounced with several bags of clothes. Lena didn't think she had to ask to come to my house or tell me how long she was staying because she was my mother. I knew I was ignoring Glenda when Lena came around and allowing Lena to disrespect her as the "Woman of the House," but I never learned how to stand up to Lena. In my family, you did not disrespect your elders or talk back no matter what, that's just how I was raised and every generation before me. Glenda would lock herself in the bedroom for the duration of Lena's stay, no matter how many weeks it was. She would only come out to eat then she would go back to the bedroom. When Glenda walked through the house, Lena would stare at her as if she was the uninvited guest in her son's house.

One day, Glenda came up the hall to brew her coffee, and she sat down at the kitchen table. I didn't realize Glenda was watching me, as I looked at Lena when she got up and walked over to the door, like I always did. Lena turned and looked at Glenda with a smirk on her face. Glenda looked disgusted and confused at the same time. When Lena went to the bathroom, Glenda asked, "Why were you staring at your mother like that?" "Like what?" I asked. As if you were lusting after her. I didn't respond, because I knew it made Glenda upset. She already had me in hot water with Lena for being so rude and locking herself in the bedroom. When Lena left, Glenda and I were arguing, and she brought it to my attention that Lena probably enjoyed it when we were not speaking to each other.

Glenda had gotten a job working at the phone company. Before I knew it, we had become strangers under the same roof. We didn't talk that much anymore, she had her own money and I had mine, we just shared the same house. Glenda had started hanging with her single friend Charlene again and even spending the night with her. I missed her, but whenever she walked in the door, I acted like I was getting along just fine without her, and I wouldn't even acknowledge her presence.

One Saturday afternoon, I was home watching the football game. In between commercials, I went to put a load of clothes in the washing machine. I didn't have enough colored clothes to complete a full load, so I reached over and grabbed some of Glenda's pants. Some coins fell out of her pockets, so I checked to see if anything else was in them. I found a folded piece of yellow paper with blue lines. Thinking it might be of significance to her, I opened it up to see what was on it. It was a hand-written letter that said, "Thanks for last night, it was very special, I hope we can get together again soon." I knew that the letter did not come from Charlene. They have been friends forever, and now that they are hanging out again... there would be no need to write letters. Glenda didn't come home that night, but she was there when I got home from work the next day. At first, I wanted to ignore her and act like I didn't find the note, but this was too big for the silent treatment. She was sitting in the recliner, smoking a cigarette. I looked at her real hard, but she didn't pay me any attention. It took all I had because I didn't want her to think I cared, but I asked her if she was having an affair. She used my own tactic against me, just sitting there... ignoring me like she didn't hear a word I said. I was starting to get upset, so I walked over and leaned in towards her face. I asked her again, but she continued to ignore me. Before I knew it, I had slapped her. She grabbed her face and jumped out of the recliner as if she was in shock. "Are you crazy?" she asked. She shoved me out of the way as she headed down the hall. I didn't know what she was about to do, but I knew I didn't want her to leave and go back to whoever wrote her the letter, so I shoved her so hard that she fell into the wall and hit the floor.

Glenda started crying. When she got up from the floor, she went into the bedroom and called the police. About fifteen minutes later, there was a knock at the door. We were questioned about what had happened and I was taken into custody.

I called Uncle Daniel to get me out because I didn't want Lena to get word of this. She would go on a tangent about why I should leave Glenda, and I didn't feel like hearing it. Uncle Daniel drove down to bail me out. When I was released, I apologized for having to ask him to come so far to get me out of jail, then I told him… "Thank you." As we were leaving the Police Station to go to his car, I thought he was going to ask me what happened but instead, he stopped and put his arm around my neck, and apologized. I didn't understand what he was apologizing for. He said, "I knew this was going to happen one day, I'm just surprised it didn't happen sooner." I was still confused.

Uncle Daniel started crying and he proceeded to say, "Thank goodness I'm only bailing you out of jail, instead of visiting you in prison or the Psychiatric Ward. When you grow up in a crazy environment and that's all you know, it's easy to start accepting it as the norm, but nothing about your childhood was normal. You went through so much as a child- mental, physical, verbal abuse, and some strange stuff in between. You've been beat down by women all your life, you were bound to take those frustrations out on some woman one day. Unfortunately, it would be one who had nothing to do with all that nonsense. I should have done more than what I did when you were growing up. You are not your mother's husband and you are not Ron's father. You don't owe anybody anything... you owe it to yourself to get some help. The average person would not have made it through what you've been through. That's why I'm so proud of you. After everything you had to go through as a child, I don't even know if going in the Military was a good idea, but I understand, you had to get away. Promise me one thing- you will get some help or talk to somebody before you get into some serious trouble. You can't keep holding it in. Time doesn't heal everything. Some things just have to be dealt with." Uncle Daniel hugged me, and we stood there in front of the Police Station... hugging and crying until we had no more tears left. A few minutes later, we got in his car and he drove me home. When I got out of the car, he said, "Remember what I said." I nodded my head and closed the door.

When I went inside the house, Glenda was gone. A week later, she came back while I was watching a football game. When I saw the bruise on her face, I knew Uncle Daniel was right, I also knew my marriage was over, but I had too much pride to admit that it bothered me. At first, I acted as if I didn't even see her come inside the house. I had been ignoring women since I was a little boy, and I knew that it hurt them more than anything...but I eventually learned not to ignore a hurting woman, especially when you vowed to love and protect her.

I was pretending like I was so deep into the football game when Glenda came by me with several large boxes. I was accustomed to her packing a few things to stay overnight with Charlene, but I soon realized Glenda was moving out. She didn't care if I was ignoring her or not. I tried to strike up a conversation with her, but she wasn't interested. "So where are you moving?" I asked. Once it came out of my mouth, it sounded even more inconsiderate. She didn't even flinch. When she closed the front door, I knew she was really gone this time. My eyes filled with water as I tried to continue watching the game. When I woke up the next day, the house felt completely lifeless. I had not told anybody at work that Glenda and I had split, thankfully she had stopped working there years ago or it would be all over the warehouse by now.

A month later, I walked to the mailbox. There was a letter from a Law Office inside, with divorce papers from Glenda. Before I could get back inside the house and internalize it all, a car pulled in the driveway beside me, it was Ron and Lena. Lena was the last person I wanted to see. As soon as she got inside the house, she started complaining about how dusty and unkept everything was. "Does that woman of yours ever clean up? Where is she at anyway?" she asked, in a hateful tone. "Gone," I said, with all the strength I had left. "Well good," said Lena. "You didn't need her anyway." As far as Lena was concerned, she still thought Glenda was just my girlfriend, I never dared to tell her we were married. It didn't matter now anyway. In one of the most vulnerable times in my life, I couldn't show any weakness in the presence of Lena, so I changed the subject by boasting about how much money I had in my retirement plan. I always found myself trying to prove something to her which only got me into more trouble. Little did I know, Lena and Ron were making plans with every dime I had. I thought to myself, who asks someone to borrow against their retirement savings.

# 28

## JAKE'S ARREST

It was a Saturday morning. Roxie's side of the family was getting ready to attend a family reunion. Jake's cousin Rodney, and his family were packed and ready to walk out the door when the phone rang. When Rodney saw Jake's name on the caller I.D., he refused to answer it. He didn't want to tell Jake he was going to the family reunion because he knew he would hold him on the phone forever, telling him every reason why he shouldn't go, then he would start criticizing anybody who he thought would have anything to do with Charlotte. Jake was unable to get in touch with any of his relatives that day, so he retreated to nature. He gathered his fishing rods and went down to the lake at the edge of his property.

Jake had been fishing for about half an hour when he heard an alarm go off. Jake was startled because he lived on a large, quiet piece of property, and he had no neighbors. Jake gathered his fishing equipment and started walking back towards his house. When he got over the hill, he saw Raquel's car, but some guy had a crowbar bashing in the windows of his new red Nissan 300ZX. Jake dropped his bucket and fishing rods and started running towards his car. He grabbed Juan and started slamming his head into Raquel's car. Juan fell to the ground lifeless, and Jake continued to kick him. Raquel jumped out of the passenger seat and ran around to the side of Jake's car. When Jake realized she had brought Juan to his house, he grabbed her by the throat. All his suppressed frustrations towards Roxie and Charlotte ignited like fireworks. Jake thought about how kind he had been to Raquel, trusting her when he was warned not to, inviting her into his home and she betrayed him for somebody else. "You brought him to my house?" Jake questioned her violently. Jake didn't realize that he was choking Raquel so hard, she couldn't breathe. All his gloating with the guys about killing anybody else who crossed him the wrong way was coming to fruition. As Raquel stopped resisting and her body became limp, Jake suddenly snapped out of it. Once Jake gathered himself, he couldn't believe what he had just done. He ran inside the house and called 911 and explained everything that happened. Even though he followed the ambulance to the hospital to make sure Raquel was alright, when she became conscious enough to talk, she was questioned by the authorities, and Jake was arrested.

# 29

## LAYING DOWN THE LAW
## TOO LATE

**M**att had had enough of John and he knew it was time to deal with the demons he had created. When John reluctantly finished high school, Matt cut him off. John could live with Matt and Phoebe, but he had to buy his own clothes and provide his transportation. This news did not sit well with John. He was not used to being told no; and even worse, how was he supposed to maintain his flamboyant lifestyle? John could no longer parade around in his father's Cadillac Escalade, and he had too much pride to get a regular 9 to 5 job like the classmates he bullied and made fun of.

John woke up late one afternoon, still thinking about his new living stipulations. He was hungry, so he decided to walk over to Bob's Burger Joint. While John was waiting for his food to be prepared, he heard loud music with bass playing outside. Everybody in the line turned around to see who it was. John grabbed his food and went outside. It was Trey, driving a gold 1978 Dodge Aspen with 18' rims. It had huge speakers, an amplifier, and tweeters. The sound system was so loud that when Trey turned the volume up, the windows of the burger joint would vibrate and so would the windows of all the other cars in the parking lot. John was hoping to get his food and leave out without Trey noticing him, but Trey spotted him as soon as he stepped outside of Bob's Burger Joint. He turned the radio down and called John over to his car. John had already thought of an excuse if Trey asked why he was walking. John walked over to the car as the sun glaring off the gold paint was almost blinding from the angle which Trey had parked. Trey stepped out of the car and reached out to shake John's hand. "What's up man?" he said. "Nothing much, is this you?" replied John, referring to the nice ride that Trey had. "I'm out walking, trying to get some exercise." John was trying to figure out where Trey got so much money from, or what kind of job he had that paid him that well. "Where have you been man?" "I haven't seen you since we graduated, did you move?" Trey asked. "No, I've just been laying low. What about you?

When did you get this car? I don't remember any jobs around here paying that kind of money," said John. "Job? I don't have a job. I don't punch anybody's time clock. I work for myself." "Doing what?" "Hop in," said Trey.

John jumped in the car and they rode around the corner and down the block to a safe place where they could talk. Trey parked in an abandoned parking lot and turned the bass down. "I sell black tar," said Trey. "Black tar what?" asked John. "Black tar heroin" "Man, that's some dangerous stuff!" said John. "I'm not the one using it, I'm just selling it, you know what I'm saying?" "Yeah, I know what you're saying. If you get caught, you can get into some serious trouble too." "That's just it, I don't plan on getting caught. In less than 6 months, I was able to buy this ride, get my own place, and I got a few grand stacked at the house. Well, think about it, man. I'm not trying to pressure you into anything, it's just easy money." Trey cranked the car and backed out of the parking lot, asking John if he wanted him to take him home. John said yeah. Otherwise, he would have to walk back, and he was too ashamed to let anyone see him walking home from that side of town. When Trey got to John's parent's house, he looked over at John and said, "Just think about it, unless you got plans to go to college or something," he said sarcastically. John knew he wasn't going to college. "But if you're in the same boat as me and most of the guys from this little country town, give me a call," said Trey. John opened the car door, thinking about what Trey had said. "I appreciate the ride. I might catch up with you later," he said. John closed the car door and started walking towards the house. Trey slowly backed out of the driveway and turned up his sound system as he drove off.

For the first time, John was seeing what it felt like to have someone do him a favor and he didn't like it, it felt too much like asking for a handout. John was getting tired of being confined to the house already. The idea of fast money was starting to sound better and better and he couldn't stop thinking about Trey's new car.

# 30

## CDL LICENSE

I enrolled in a truck driving school to keep my mind busy, I figured I would become a cross country driver since Glenda was gone and I had no reason to stay around the house. Several weeks later, I graduated, earning my CDL license. I had saved enough to put a down payment on my own tractor-trailer. I was so excited about the new journey I was on, but I had not told anybody but Ken, he was my next-door neighbor. Ken was going to give me a ride to the dealership when I was got ready to purchase the rig.

I was watching TV on a Friday afternoon when Ron called. I was hesitant to tell him the good news, but I thought, what the heck. He congratulated me, then he asked, "What company will you drive for? "I haven't narrowed my decision down yet, but I know I'll be purchasing my own rig." "How are you going to do that?" he asked. "I've been putting money aside for a while." To my surprise, Ron suggested we should go to Jolynn's on Saturday to celebrate. I thought to myself, "Why not," after all, it had been years since I ate at Jolynn's.

Saturday morning, I was getting ready to go next door and have Ken take me to the dealership. Just as I grabbed my jacket and keys, I heard a knock at the front door. I wasn't expecting anybody that early, so I went to see who it was. When I opened the door, it was Ron. He was wearing a wardrobe that I could never afford or at least, I was too conservative to spend that kind of money on. His shoes alone cost $200. Ron always wore high-end attire. I invited him in, but before I could ask him why he came so early, he mentioned he was on a tight schedule and he had to hurry and get back. I was thinking to myself, why did he come if he was in such a hurry, but I kept my thoughts to myself. Since Ron had arrived so early and was rushing to get back to his house, I called the dealership to let them know I would be there much later and I called Ken to let him know I had a change of plans. I didn't want to be in a rush when I made my selection.

It took us a while to get to Jolynn's. When we arrived,

I wanted to splurge, but I didn't because I assumed Ron was paying, even though he never had before. So, I got the special of the day which was the Rib-eye steak, mashed potatoes, and green beans. Ron wasn't quite ready to order yet. He asked the waitress to give him a few more minutes. I told him I would be back, I needed to use the restroom. When I got back, my food was already on the table. "What took you so long?" Ron asked. I thought I was going to have to come and get you." "The soap dispenser was empty, and they didn't have enough paper towels," I said. "I bet you spent half the time looking in the mirror too... just like Lena, didn't you?" Ron joked. The waitress came to see if I needed anything else to drink, but Ron's food still wasn't ready. A few minutes later, three waitresses came out of the kitchen with three plates and a bowl. I thought to myself.... wow! Somebody sure did order a lot of food. The first waitress stopped at our table and put down a plate of fried shrimp, fish, hush puppies, and fries then she stepped aside. The second waitress put down a plate of lasagna and a side salad. Before I could tell the third waitress that we didn't order all that food, I noticed Ron wasn't saying a word, he was busy making room for the other food that was coming. The last platter had a steak, baked potato, and sautéed broccoli. I immediately lost my appetite. Whenever Ron is not paying for the food, he orders as much as he can. He and Lena always assume that I have money without asking. I fell for the old, "We need to go celebrate" and I would be footing the bill, even though I was the honoree." Ron was on the heavy side, but he ordered enough food that would last me three days. He needed two take-out boxes for his entrees alone. When we got back to the house, Ron invited himself in. Personally, I was ready for him to leave.

Ron sat down and started telling jokes. Whenever he wanted to ask for something, he tried to put me in a good mood with funny stories about his friends or childhood memories, but he forgot, my childhood memories weren't as delightful as his. I went into the kitchen and started straightening up while he kept babbling on and on. Ron got quiet, then he came into the kitchen where I was and he said, "All jokes aside Timothy, I need that money that you saved up. It took me a while, but I finally got a job at Trevor's Uniforms. They make work uniforms and package them, but I drive a forklift and move the finished product to the shipping dock. While I was waiting to get hired, my rent got behind and now, I'm being evicted. I found another apartment, but I need the down payment and first month's rent to move in." At that moment, there was a war going on in my head, I could not believe what I was hearing. Yes, I was glad he finally got a real job and had stopped all the side-street hustling. Perhaps, he might be able to pay me back this time. On the other hand, I was fed up with giving him money, especially after that stunt he pulled at Jolynn's. At the same time, I didn't want Lena showing up and beating my door down because I didn't give him the money, and I certainly didn't want him thinking about moving in with me.

# 31

## THE SENTENCING

Raquel and Juan survived, but Jake had some serious charges against him, and a couple of the counts pertained to attempts to murder. His charges were so severe that he had to remain in jail until his court date. Laverne had to become Jakes Power of Attorney, and that wouldn't be the first of his grandfather's ideologies that he would have to scrap from his list of rules regarding women. Laverne having total access to every dime Jake had was the least of his worries now. Laverne got Jake the best attorney that money could buy. Jake didn't get the amount of time that he was facing, but he was sentenced to serve twenty years, due to the nature of his offense. He could be released in eight years with good behavior. Jake was moved from Meadow Creek City Jail to a high-security prison in South Alabama.

Jake's first week in prison was traumatizing to the point of contemplating suicide. I don't know what he experienced in there…I just know he wanted to get out bad. It has been said that when someone makes it out of prison alive, that's all that matters, and they don't talk about the things that took place on the inside. Jake never realized how valuable his freedom was, until now. He got his macho attitude under control immediately, because he knew prison was not the place to try to prove his manhood. There were five hundred inmates inside the institution and Jake's sanity was being put to the test daily. He wasn't very intimidating by himself. For the first time in his adult life, he had to listen and take commands from someone else. He had to go to bed, get up, eat, and shower when he was told to do so. His food was prepared by some rotten tooth, sweaty guy with dirty fingernails named Big Moe. Jake would be glad to cook his own food now, instead of harassing Laverne. Jake lost 10 lbs. during the first week. He refused to eat, causing his immune system to weaken and the temperature in the prison was so cold that he got sick. Jake had no problem keeping his egotistical opinions to himself now, unlike when he was around family and friends on the outside.

An older guy named Larry with salt and pepper hair,

noticed Jake when he arrived. It would be several weeks before he would speak to him though. Larry needed time to sum him up, to see if he was worth wasting his time on. Larry was a part of a Christian group, they had Bible Study in the Chapel, they also prayed and encouraged one another. One day, Jake was eating alone, and Larry came over to introduce himself. He asked him about his faith. Jake told him he wasn't a religious person. Larry invited Jake to come to their Bible Study anyway. Jake figured, if it will help maintain his sanity, why not, even if he didn't believe in any of it. Once Jake incorporated himself as part of the group, he realized they were some pretty good guys, even though they were in prison. They were nothing like the Christians his grandfather had described to him. Jake's new friends embraced and protected him by warning him about the troublemakers. They didn't judge him, neither did they care what he had done, they made him feel just as welcome to the group as anybody else. Jake's money had no value in this group.

Confined to a 6 by 8 ft. cell, Jake had plenty of time to think. Now, all the people whom he had offended became so dear to him. Jake started praying and meditating on scriptures every time he sensed anxiety coming on. When he was given the opportunity to make his first phone call, he spoke with Ralph. Ralph warned him not to take anything from anyone inside the prison. Ralph was aware of the personal events that lead Jake to prison, and he knew Jake could handle himself on the streets, but he knew it took a special kind of cleverness and wit to make it out of prison. After all, Ralph had spent 8 months in another institution for domestic violence. He started becoming hostile towards women during his early twenties, but the system taught him that he had to get his temper under control, and to keep his hands off of women.

A few months after Jake was completely settled into prison, he was expecting a visit from Ralph and Laverne. The security check was grueling, after all, Jake was in a facility with criminals who had committed serious crimes. After a two hour wait, Ralph and Laverne were at the front of the line. One more checkpoint and they would go to the visiting room where Jake was waiting. Jake had never been so happy to see Laverne and Ralph in his life. When Ralph saw Jake, he hugged him so tight, that they both started crying. Laverne hugged Jake too, but she didn't have much to say. Ralph and Laverne knew Jake was struggling in prison, they tried to act like they didn't notice how much weight he had lost, as he was almost unrecognizable. Laverne told him how much money she had put on his account. Ralph reminded him to keep to himself, not to take anything from anybody, and to stay away from troublemakers. "If they do something crazy and pull you in it, you will get punished too," he said. Jake had been there three months now, but it seemed like 3 years. The visit had lasted 25 minutes, but to Jake, it felt as if only 5 minutes had elapsed. A guard came and told them they had 5 more minutes. Sundays were the shortest visiting days. Ralph and Laverne stood up and gave Jake one last hug. "It won't be long, just try to stay positive, I will send you some paper too, so you can write us," said Ralph. After they said their final good-byes, Ralph and Laverne exited the room and went back in the direction they came from. The prison guard didn't give Jake a chance to watch them leave.

After a year had passed, Jake was ready to attend counseling. Anger management therapy was a part of his sentencing. Since he had been going to Chapel with the Christian group, he opted for a Christian Counselor. On Day 1 of counseling, Dr. Flay, a middle-aged Caucasian man, invited Jake into his office and told him how the sessions would be directed. Dr. Flay assured Jake that the session was confidential unless he revealed harming himself or someone else in the past or near future. Dr. Flay told Jake he would pray with him if he wanted to, before or at the end of the sessions. Jake nodded his head and agreed to the terms, it wasn't like he had a choice, the medium for which he would be released was to prove that he had acquired the ability to control his anger. Jake didn't have anything to say at first, he was waiting on a prompt from Dr. Flay. "So…Jake," said Dr. Flay, reassuring himself of Jake's name by glancing at his files. "Tell me a little about yourself. What do you enjoy doing?" Jake laid back in the chair and said, "I like hunting, fishing, you know…outdoor stuff." Jake proceeded to tell Dr. Flay how many deer he had killed, then he said, "You know…. I do have my own house and I do have money in the bank, unlike a lot of people in here." Dr. Flay knew that Jake was clearly trying to distinguish himself from the rest of the inmates as he didn't want to be stereotyped. Jake tried to brush over the real reason why he was there as he boasted on his own intellectual abilities. He even attempted to place himself on the same professional level as Dr. Flay. "You know…before I got in here, I use to give people advice all the time," he said. "Is that right?" "Yes, it was up to them to take heed to it though." "And how did that go?" asked Dr. Flay. "I just say what's on my mind" "Did those people like you giving them advice?" "Sometimes yeah and sometimes no, but that's just the way I am, I tell people about themselves whether they like it or not. I'm just trying to help them." Dr. Flay nodded his head and smiled. During the first session, Jake basically gave his own narrative. "Well Jake, it was nice meeting and talking with you today. Unfortunately, our hour is about to end," said Dr. Flay. They both stood up and shook hands. Dr. Flay put away Jake's files and started preparing for the next appointment and Jake was escorted back to his cell.

When Jake came to counseling the next week, Dr. Flay felt confident that he would be able to help him, in fact, he was looking forward to seeing Jake, as he had positive expectations of the session. Dr. Flay asked Jake how he was feeling. Jake responded, "Pretty good," Then Dr. Flay did a brief reflection on what had taken place during the previous counseling session. He noticed that even though Jake acted as if he had it all together, he had lost a significant amount of weight prior to his mug shot on entry day. Dr. Flay decided that he would prompt Jake to talk about what lead to his arrest. Otherwise, if Jake kept boasting about his self-accomplishments, they would never get anywhere. "So... Jake, I understand that you are a smart guy, and you've worked hard to achieve everything that you have, but could you tell me about the events that led you here?" Jake paused; he was completely out of his element. For the first time, he was under the microscope...

where his deepest pains and emotions were about to be dissected.

Jake was starting to let down his guard, feeling as though another self-entitled accolade had been stripped from him. Jake came to the realization that his "life accomplishments and all-knowing attitude" meant nothing to Dr. Flay or anybody else in prison. Jake was quiet at first, then he tilted his head to the side, and then back vertical – as if a deep thought had been dropped into the top of his head. Jake sat up straight, then he leaned in towards Dr. Flay with his elbows resting on his thighs and his fingers clenched in between one another. He let out a deep breath and said, "You know... you give a woman everything you got, but they don't care. You go to work all day and you come home and she got some old nasty man laying up in the house that you paid for." Dr. Flay kept a calm face, but he knew he was getting somewhere. The things that Jake said were surprising, but Dr. Flay had to maintain a body posture that would keep Jake in a state of flow. "One thing for sure, I will never put my name on a house with another woman again," said Jake. Dr. Flay had to grab his pencil and journal as he felt Jake was honestly pouring out his heart. At the end of the session, he stood up and shook hands with Jake and said, "Today was a good

session, I really feel like we are moving towards progress."
Jake silently nodded in agreement, realizing that counseling
was starting to give him a sense of relief, then the guard
outside the door came to escort him back to his cell.

When Jake left, Dr. Flay turned to his desk and looked
at Jake's files - to see if he was married. He saw that Jake
had never been married and during his gloating episodes,
he made a point to inform Dr. Flay that he owns his own
house, vehicles, property and he had a lot of money in the
bank. What Jake was disclosing didn't line up with the
charges and accusations in his arrest record.

The next week during counseling, Dr. Flay prompted
Jake to continue where he previously left off. Jake paused
for a minute then he said, "Oh yeah, all women do the same
thing, none of them are any good. They just want you for
your money and what you can give them. Then they turn on
you." Dr. Flay thought to himself, I have to find out who
this mysterious woman is because she seems to be the root
of all Jake's frustrations. "Do you mind talking a little bit
more about this woman? Or is it several women?" "No, it's
just one, but yeah... I can tell you about her." "Was it an old
girlfriend?" asked Dr. Flay. "No," said Jake. Dr. Flay was
thinking maybe Jake lost trust in women at an early age,
due to manipulation and he became a magnet for the same

kind of women throughout his life, which had led to animosity and distrust towards all women. As Jake continued to disclose, he would soon drop a surprise on Dr. Flay. "I grew up close to my mother," Jake continued. "All my life, she led me to believe that I was the most important person in her life. She started calling me her "Little Man," after our father walked out on us." "I can imagine that made you feel very special and important at such a young age," said Dr. Flay. "Yes," Jake replied." "I had an older brother, but I was the MAN of the house. My mother dealt with sorry useless guys as far back as I could remember. I started working in high school to help make ends meet. After high school, I got a better job and I bought her a new car and built her a new house. The house was in both of our names even though I paid the mortgage." I worked from sunup to sundown; every day, providing a roof over her head. Sometimes when I got home from work, I couldn't even talk to her because there was always some guy laying across her bed. They never offered her anything worth-while or bothered to take care of her as I did. None of her other children took care of her either. She had it good though because I made sure she didn't want for anything."

"One day, I got into it with her daughter. "Why do you refer to your sister as your mother's daughter?" "Because she's no sister of mine. She caused me to get arrested and because she was really my mother's favorite, she chose her daughter over me when I went to court… like I didn't mean anything to her." Dr. Flay completely understood what Jake was dealing with now. When Jake finished explaining everything that had happened to him, and how he felt about the situation, Dr. Flay began to design his next sessions around forgiveness and letting go.

Nearing the final sessions, Dr. Flay issued Jake the homework assignment of inviting his mother to join him as though she was still alive, the same way he would sit with her on the bed when he was younger. He was to confess to her all his hurts, unforgiveness, everything he did for her that she did not appreciate, and everything she did that hurt him. Then he was to ask for forgiveness for being angry at her for so long and he was to forgive her for the pain she caused him. Since Jake was so sensitive to the topic and he didn't want to expose his vulnerabilities in front of his inmate, he was granted special permission to go to the Chapel. Jake sat on a pew in the back corner by himself. Instead of talking, he chose to write a three-page letter to Roxie, pouring out his heart in its entirety. Jake shed a lot of tears during the process, causing the lines on the paper to fade. At the end of the letter, he signed, P.S. I forgive you…I'm not your "Little Man" anymore, because I refuse to remain trapped in the disappointments and bitterness of my youth, but I am Jake Jones… a broken, but healing "Grown Man."

When Jake got back to his cell, he ripped the letter up and flushed it down the toilet. That night, while lying on his bunk, Jake felt stronger than he ever had in his life, without having to belittle anyone else. He was finally gaining control over his emotions. His new-found inner strength gave him what he needed to endure the rest of his time in prison. Jake felt motivated enough to take some classes and learn a new trade.

The next time Ralph came to visit Jake, he came alone. Jake was still on the small side, but his weight was coming back. Ralph could tell by talking to Jake that he was going to be all right.

# 32

## JAKE'S RELEASE

Today was the day that Jake would be going home. His Christian brothers prayed for his safety after release and that he would make good decisions and stay out of trouble. When Jake walked through the last door, Ralph was waiting at the entrance, but Laverne was nowhere in sight. Jake hugged Ralph. He didn't care how long the ride home was, he was just glad to be free. Jake started telling Ralph how bad the prison food was and how he couldn't wait to get one of Jolynn's greasy cheeseburgers with bacon, extra pickles, and two orders of fresh-cut fries. Jake wanted to go to Randall's for a large chocolate ice cream soda too. Ralph warned him to take it easy, and that his stomach would have to readjust to the outside food.

After several hours on the road, Ralph pulled over at

Jolynn's and they ordered everything Jake requested. Some members of Matt's church were there. Jake didn't know how they were going to act towards him, but once they realized who he was, they came over to tell him they were glad to see him. Jake was instantly reminded of how he despised Christianity prior to going to prison and how the Chapel Priest taught him that humans don't have the right to judge anyone else, only God can do that. He remembered how the Christians embraced him in prison and taught him to love and forgive.

The waitress that took their order wore a name tag that read, Maggie. She had dark skin, a pretty bright smile, her hair was naturally curly, and she wore burgundy lipstick. She was from the Islands. Jake liked her accent, which was uncommon in Meadow Brook. She recanted their order and told them she would be right back with their food.

Jake was so glad to see a pretty woman, then he thought about Lavern. "What happened to Lavern," he asked Ralph? "I don't know, she knew it was your release day. I tried to call her, but I didn't get an answer." Jake thought to himself, that's odd. Laverne was always there for him no matter what, even when he was disrespectful to her in the past, not that he was proud of his previous behavior. Several bites into his entrée, his stomach started making strange sounds and he told Ralph they might need to wrap it up and head towards the house. Ralph started laughing. "I told you. You got to slowly introduce this food back into your system."

Ralph drove Jake home to use the restroom. When Ralph pulled into Jake's driveway, there sat his new red Nissan 300ZX, bashed in, under a blue tarp. A lot of bad emotions started flooding back to Jake's memory, but he didn't have time to relive them, he had to get to the restroom fast. When Jake came out of the restroom, he went to get some clothes so he could take a shower. He noticed the house looked abandoned, as if Laverne had not been there in months. After he got a shower, he laid across the bed and took a nap.

Jake woke up about an hour later and called Laverne. As he was dialing her number, he noticed there was a stack of papers on the coffee table beside the phone base. After several rings, Laverne's voicemail came on and Jake hung up. He picked up the papers on the table and looked at them. They were receipts for his lawyer fees and money that was put on his account while he was in prison. Later that week, Jake went to the bank, he checked his account and matched every receipt. He realized just how good of a person Laverne was. She could have taken him for everything he had, but she had not taken any more money from his account than what was spent on him. She paid his land taxes each year and his utilities with her own money, even though she moved out about a year before Jake was released.

Later that night, Ralph called to check on Jake, and he told him where his girlfriend said Laverne had moved to. Jake worked out that night and decided to make a surprise visit to Laverne's house the next day.

When the next day came, Jake put on some nice clothes and the cologne that Laverne liked for him to wear. He got in his pickup and drove to where Ralph told him she had moved. As he drove down the street, he spotted Laverne's little black Mazda, but he also noticed another vehicle beside it that he didn't recognize. It was a diesel truck, something told him it didn't belong to any of Laverne's friends. Jake kept going past the house and turned around in the cul-de-sac. When he came back passed Laverne's house, he didn't bother to look that way, he continued to look straight ahead until he reached the entrance of the subdivision, then he drove back home.

Jake couldn't sit in the house every day, doing nothing, so he applied for a Job at U.S. Locomotives. Within three days, he was called in for an interview. Jake's supervisor liked him a lot, he was a hard worker and he kept to himself. Jake had a new appreciation for freedom and independence, but more than anything, he had learned how to keep from imposing on the freedoms of others. Several months had passed and he still had not heard from Laverne. At this point, Jake just wanted to apologize, he didn't care if she didn't want to have anything else to do with him.

One day, Jake went to Jolynn's on his lunch break. Maggie came to his table with the same bright smile and burgundy lipstick. Jake ordered a BLT and a soda. Just as Maggie was bringing his food, he noticed a lady outside. She appeared to harass the other guys as they came inside the restaurant for lunch. He wanted to get a better look at the woman. When Maggie noticed what Jake was staring at, she peered through the window while placing his plate on the table. "Do you know who that lady is," he asked. "You don't want to know her," she said. "She comes here sometimes around lunchtime to harass the workers. I think she's homeless."

Jake didn't want to say it out loud, but the woman looked so familiar to him. Maggie turned and walked away to refill some of the other customer's drinks. Jake kept looking at the woman and she finally turned around, facing the restaurant window, but because of the bright sun glare reflecting off the glass, she could not see Jake sitting inside. Just then, he realized the frail woman with long-thinning hair like his mother and missing teeth was Charlotte. Jake instantly had a flashback from Chapel. "We don't have to play God, he sees to it, that people reap what they sow." Jake not only forgave Roxie in prison, but he eventually forgave Charlotte as well. Jake drank most of his soda, but he didn't have an appetite to eat his sandwich. As Jake got up from the table, Maggie said with an Island accent, "You Americans waste so much food. Why do you order so much if you are not going to eat it, American Man?" Even though Maggie was being sarcastic, Jake liked the sound of Maggie calling him a man, not a little man, just a real American Man… with no strings attached. He wanted to entertain Maggie's comment, but he had so many thoughts rushing through his mind and he had to get back to work. Jake asked Maggie for a to-go box. When she brought it back, he placed the sandwich inside and closed it. Jake asked Maggie if she would give the box to the lady outside. Then he reached inside his wallet to leave Maggie a $5 tip and he pulled out three twenty-dollar bills, folded them up, and asked if she would give them to the lady too. Maggie looked at him with a questionable look on her face and said, "Are you sure? "Yes," and he got up and walked out of the restaurant. Maggie went outside and gave Charlotte the food and money. Charlotte looked at her and said, "Thank you." "Don't thank me, it's from him" said Maggie, as she pointed to the edge of the parking lot at Jake, as he was getting into his old Ford pick-up truck. Jake never looked back while he was pulling out of the parking lot. Charlotte studied the truck and the back of the driver's head. After a few seconds, she knew exactly who it was. She just stood there staring... until the truck turned into a little speck in the distance.

When Jake got home that night, he worked out. He couldn't get the bad image of Charlotte out of his mind. He was reminded of something Dr. Flay told him in counseling. "It hurts you more to hold grudges against others. When you forgive them, you are released from the stronghold that keeps you in the mental bondage tied to them." For the first time in his life, Jake said a prayer for Charlotte before he went to bed. Jake didn't go back to Jolynn's for a while, but Charlotte never showed up there again.

# 33

## JOHN'S NEW ENDEAVORS

John was working with one of his friends now, at least, that's what Matt thought. John was getting up every morning around the same time and coming back home in the afternoons at the same time. Before long, he had his own car, but he was wearing expensive clothes that he should not have been able to afford. Matt thought maybe he had so much money because he didn't have the bills that most adults had.

It was a Friday night, Matt and Phoebe had finished watching a movie and they were getting ready for bed. John was still out with his friends and they figured he would be in later.

Matt and Phoebe had been asleep for about an hour when the phone rang. Matt was alarmed by the phone call.

The last time he received a call in the middle of the night, it was Mother Wells who lived beside the church. She was calling to let him know that the kitchen in the old church had caught fire. Matt would soon find out it was a collect call from John, he was at Meadow Brook Police Department and the operator was asking if Matt would accept the charges. When Matt accepted the charges, John told him he had been arrested and he needed someone to get him out of jail. Matt didn't ask any questions over the phone, he told John he would be right there, and he hung up. Matt didn't want to worry Phoebe, but she rolled over and asked who was on the phone. Matt told her John had been arrested but not to worry, he was going to see what had happened. Phoebe got up, there was no way she could fall back asleep now.

All the way to the jail, Matt tried to figure out what had happened, he thought there must have been a mistake. Matt had never been arrested in his life and now his son was in jail. When Matt arrived at the jail, he was told the crime that John had committed and the serious charges that he was facing. John had sold black tar heroin to an undercover Police Officer outside a night club. Matt could not believe what he was hearing. After speaking with the Criminal Investigator, he was upset, but he knew he needed a lawyer and a lot of money fast, to prevent John from going to prison. Matt had spoiled John and he knew John would never survive any amount of time in prison.

According to the church bylaws, John's transgressions would prove that Matt was failing at governing his own household. Therefore, the church was the last place that Matt wanted to turn to. Before this incident, Matt had been a good pastor and he had never given anyone a reason to doubt his trustworthiness. When Matt took over the church in the place of Reverend Wells, he took bartering services in the form of payment. He was not given a generous wage contract until the church started growing and the tithes and offerings became abundant.

Matt spent several days contemplating what he was going to do about John's trial, he needed roughly $18,000 to get a good lawyer, pay all the court fees, and keep John from going to prison. Matt remembered that he served as the Treasurer many years prior to becoming pastor of the church, and he still had access to the church bank account which somehow slipped passed Mr. Fitzgerald.

For the first time, Matt was starting to have resentment towards Marie. He felt the struggles of his childhood blindsided him when it came to rearing his own son. His sermons began to change, as the focus was on helping others and being able to keep secrets, which many members found perplexing.

Matt was at his wit's end, so he requested to meet with the Board of Trustees one Sunday after service. This was the hardest thing he ever had to do, he had always been responsible, even as a child and he never had to ask for handouts from anyone. During the meeting, Matt said he needed to borrow a large sum of money, but he wouldn't say what it was for. The four trustees were split. Deacon Sherman and Mrs. Blakely thought Matt was good on his word while Mr. Fitzgerald and Deacon Wade took into consideration the generous wage contract that he was just given, the current mortgage payment of the church, and they didn't feel comfortable giving him that kind of money without knowing what it was for. Mr. Fitzgerald was not the Christian type who spread brotherly love, he was more interested in church politics and controlling the finances. Whatever Mr. Fitzgerald said, Deacon Wade agreed with it.

Matt was at his breaking point. He couldn't get all the trustees to come to an agreement, but John's court date and lawyer fees were fast approaching. Matt searched for the church bank account information in the file cabinet at his home office. When he found the check book, he wrote a check to himself in the amount of $18,000 and went downtown to the Meadow Brook Community Bank. When Matt arrived, he was just as confident and serious as ever about the business at hand. Matt stepped up to the teller. "How can I help you?" she asked. "I would like to have this check deposited into my account," replied Matt. The teller recognized Matt from making deposits and doing personal business. He had already forged Deacon Sherman and Mrs. Blakely's signature on the check. He needed one more, which was his own. The teller got up and walked to the back. Matt stood there just as calm as he would - if he were writing a check from his own bank account. When the teller came back, she handed Matt the deposit receipt, and asked if there was anything else she could help him with. "That will be all. Thank you," said Matt, and he walked out of the bank.

Matt's plan was to go back to work and start repaying the money, his distorted thinking fooled him to think that he could replace the money before anybody realized it was missing.

# 34

## JOHN'S COURT DATE

**M**att and Phoebe went to court with John - without the church ever knowing about it. Matt's sacrifice had paid off, at least for now. John walked away with 10 years of probation and no jail time since it was his first offense. The only thing Matt cared about was John not having to go to prison, but little did he know, his sacrifice would land him back in court in a matter of time.

Meanwhile, Matt's dishonesty would soon be found out. Mr. Fitzgerald worked in the Finance Department at Meadow Brook Community Bank, but he's hardly ever seen in the lobby. His office is down a long hall and in the last room on the right. Mr. Fitzgerald secretly checks the church account about once a month to make sure everything is accurate. One day during lunchtime, the temperature outside was soaring in the upper 90's, so Mr. Fitzgerald decided to stay in and get a bag of chips out of the vending machine from the breakroom. When he returned to his desk, he decided to log into his computer and check on the church account. After Mr. Fitzgerald saw where Deacon Wade had deposited the money from Sunday's service. To his surprise, he saw a large withdrawal from weeks prior. Mr. Fitzgerald thought for sure he was mistaken, so he refreshed the screen, but the account continued to yield the same results. Mr. Fitzgerald knew his computer needed upgrading but he thought a serious technical error had occurred this time. He could not accept what he was seeing, so he shut the computer down and restarted it. He had no idea who could have received that kind of money from the church without any of the trustees signing on it. Mr. Fitzgerald decided to write down the date of the transaction and check the cameras in the bank. When he reviewed the surveillance recordings, he could not believe what he saw. After a few minutes of focusing, he was able to determine that the man standing in front of the teller, wearing black slacks and white shirt, was Matt. Mr. Fitzgerald was furious, he called Deacon Wade and the other members of the board to tell them what he had discovered. The Trustees didn't believe him at first, they thought there must have been mistake. With evidence, they would soon accept there was no mistake.

After Matt finished preaching the following Sunday morning, the Trustees called a meeting with him. Matt admitted to taking the money, but he still wouldn't say why. He also told them he was in the process of paying it back. Standing in front of the board brought back the same emotions he experienced as a child, when the ladies at the church would whisper and stare at his mother and all her fatherless children.

Matt tried to live a perfect life, he preached convicting sermons that put the fear of God in his congregation every week. His teachings provoked repentance and he cautioned members about intentionally sinning or offending others - for there would be great consequences in the end. The church was growing rapidly with roughly 1,500 active members, the making of the first Mega Church in the small town of Meadow Brook. Who would have ever thought that when the shoe was on the other foot, Matt would not be able to admit his own faults?

After a long discussion between the five of them, Mr. Fitzgerald and Deacon Wade decided they should have Matt removed from the church, for fear that he was not trustworthy.  The trustee Board scheduled a conference with all the members of the church the following week.

Deacon Wade opened the meeting by thanking everyone who came then he proceeded to explain the findings and accusations against Matt. As fate would have it, the church was divided. Some 70% of the members were with Matt. They loved him - no matter what he did, they knew he was a Godly man and something bad must have happened for him to have done what he did. 20% wanted him to tell the church why he took the money, which Matt was not willing to do, he had preached too many sermons about how other people should raise their children. 10% despised Matt, and just wanted him to leave. They believed all preachers would steal from the church if given the chance.

In the past, Matt helped so many people to the point that Phoebe thought they were going to come up short paying their own bills. He would give money to the less fortunate when the Trustee Board refused to. Matt loaned people money to buy groceries, pay their bills, even medical bills. If everybody paid him back all the money owed to him, he would not have had to borrow that money from the church. I remember Matt telling me and Jake that church members don't think pastors should get paid anything, but they believe pastors should always have money to lend them when they need it, and they should never have to pay them back.

# 35

## TRUTHS REVEALED

Just as the Trustee Board could not agree on whether to loan Matt the money, neither could the church collectively decide what actions should be taken against him. Mr. Fitzgerald thought Matt should be held accountable for his actions, if not, it could happen again, so he and Deacon Wade filed a lawsuit to have Matt removed from the church.

When the court date came, only a few members took off work to attend. Jake and I went to support Matt. The opposing Attorney's drilled him. They exposed every embarrassing thing about Matt, even things that we didn't know. We knew that Matt was very smart in school, and he could have become anything that he wanted, but he always had to take time off from school to help his mother. He started going to Seminary School around the time he met

Phoebe and he was going to graduate that year, but after they got married and started their family, he quit working with his uncle to find a better fulltime job, causing him to have to take off from school too. Matt intended to go back, but he never found the time. Matt never obtained any other education beyond high school. Cross-examination proved that he taught himself a lot about the Bible, Politics, Medical and Scientific Terminology, and other advanced vocabularies that he often articulated when he preached and spoke with Dignitaries and Civil Rights leaders. Matt's intellectual abilities afforded him to fluently communicate in any setting.

This was bad, we never saw Matt in such a vulnerable predicament. Matt sat there with his head down the whole time, he appeared to have aged 20 years within that year. Many of his church members had written letters, signed petitions, and said good things about him. They wrote about how he would visit them in the hospital, loan them money to pay their bills, buy them food, and they were never able to pay him back. There must have been an angel in the courtroom influencing the judge on his behalf. Since most of the members wanted Matt to remain pastor of the church, the judge granted him that right without having to reveal why he took the money but he was ordered to set up a repayment plan.

The members who wanted Matt to pay the money back and leave were some of the wealthiest members in the church. They were upset about the court ruling, so they left the church. When they left, so did their families. The congregation started to dwindle, as the truths revealed about Matt in court started to circulate throughout the congregation. People weren't attending church as much anymore, and the funds started to dwindle as well. The church was down to several hundred members. As the years went by, they couldn't afford to pay for cleaning services anymore, the roof started to leak, and the air conditioning units needed replacing.

Matt was fortunate to return to Vintage Oats at a lower position and wage. He was paying the money back at first, like the judge ordered him to, but he eventually stopped because he was no longer receiving a wage and he was putting more money in the church to keep it functioning. Over time, Matt's sermons became bitter and hateful towards the congregation, he figured people could give more than what they were giving. The church was barely bringing in enough money to pay the monthly mortgage and utilities.

When Matt started pastoring the church, he would pray

for people and they would be healed, he would prophesy blessings and healings, and it would come to past. That wasn't the case anymore, as his animosity continued to grow. The members started to realize that his prayers weren't being answered anymore, neither did his prophecies come to past as if God's anointing no longer resided with him. He no longer operated in any of his gifts. The people that Matt helped the most, left the church as well, using his actions as an excuse to walk away without repaying money they owed him.

Over time, Matt started developing anxiety and paranoia. Every time he saw someone whispering in the church, he thought they were talking about him. If it was a group of people, he thought they were plotting against him. His paranoia turned into a mild form of schizophrenia. Matt had cameras installed all over the church and inside the sanctuary. He would sit in his office and monitor each camera. If he saw two or more people talking, he addressed what he assumed they were talking about in his sermons. The members soon learned to stay out of view of the cameras or only talk to one another in the parking lot, far away from the church. Certain doors were locked that led to the direction of his office, and only his family members were permitted to proceed through them. Old members continued to fluctuate back and forth between Meadowbrook and several other churches, trying to find the right place to settle. Through Matt's sermons, he told the current members that they shouldn't communicate the church business to the old members when they came back to visit. Each remaining member had the responsibility to sponsor a fundraiser or event to help pay for the church expenses, which soon grew tiresome.

After several years of financial hardship at the church, Matt came up with the idea that if he replaced the old members with new members who didn't know the history of the church fall-out, the church could start over. Matt started removing people from their positions, or simply saying mean things to them during his sermons to make them leave on their own. New members continued to join...but not in the numbers that they did in the past. The church was down to about 100 members. Matt was beginning to realize that his plan had backfired. The remaining members started telling the new members what had happened, and they would soon leave too. Matt got to the point where he didn't trust anyone, so he placed his wife over the church finances and she soon embodied the same spirit, not knowing who to trust.

John had too much shame and guilt to come back to

the church, it meant he had to face his father's dying legacy and acknowledge that he was the cause of it. Over the years, many of the old members continued to circulate back to the church because the other churches just didn't have the same feel and level of teaching. Matt was still the most fluent Bible teacher in the community, whenever he wasn't angry. When old members returned and fellowshipped for several Sundays consistently, Matt would acknowledge their presence to make them feel like all was forgiven, but after he thought they were settled in, he would hurl insults, trying to make them feel bad for leaving and they would soon leave again. I don't know as much about the Bible as Matt, but I believe things would turn around if he repented, released his anger, and made an open confession to the old and new members about why he took the money from the bank. Unfortunately, I believe Matt has convinced himself that everybody is wrong but him.

# 36

## A TURN FOR THE BETTER

Since I couldn't purchase my tractor-trailer, I got a job driving for a local company. One day I had a large delivery for the local bakery. When I arrived, there was a plumbing van blocking the entrance, so I went around to the side door. When I went inside, there was a plumber working on the pipes that had flooded the floor. I was reminded of when I was in the Army and our showers would get clogged. I thought it was interesting how backed-up pipes were such a pain, but somebody with the right tools could come in and unclog or replace the pipes in a matter of time, and everything would work fine again. I asked the guy who was working on our shower if there was any money in plumbing, and he said, "Yeah, but the real money is in Commercial Plumbing." I had not thought about that conversation since I left the military. When I got home, I sat down in the den and looked at a brochure that I had gotten from the local community college a few years ago when I was trying to figure out what I was going to do with my life. The college offered plumbing classes for 24 months. I knew this was what I wanted to do, and not just drive trucks to keep my mind off my miserable life and failed marriage. I enrolled for the following semester. Driving during the day, and going to class at night, I finished in no time. When I started working as a plumber, I enjoyed it so much that I wanted to continue my education and become a Master Plumber. Before long, I had my license and was my own boss.

Life is finally starting to look up for me, despite everything I've been through. My job requires me to work a lot, but it is rewarding financially and psychologically - to finally have an occupation that I love. My business has expanded to the point that I have a 12-man crew and I'm getting ready to open my second office in Birmingham. My new financial freedom has afforded me to buy a new truck. I thought it would feel good to spend money on myself, but every time I do, I feel an overwhelming guilt as if I'm hoarding my own money to myself. When I take my new clothes out of the closet and try them on, I take them back off and hang them up. I've gotten in a habit of not letting anybody see me wearing anything new, for fear that they will think I have money… and start asking for it.

I never talked to a counselor like Uncle Daniel suggested, I don't know if I can ever talk to anybody about what I've been through. Some things will just have to go to the grave with me. I know that time doesn't heal everything, but distance helps a lot. I haven't talked to Lena or Ron in over a year because I stay on the road all the time. Some of my jobs require me to travel long distances out of town and I stay overnight. Whenever I get back in town, my answering machine is full of messages from Lena and Ron. They even tried to get Cindy to call with alarming messages, which did not seem like her character at all. Since I was much older than Cindy, we sort of grew up apart, so we are not that close, but she turned out okay. Uncle Daniel knows how to reach me on my pager - if there's a real emergency. I had a stack of letters from Lena that I had never opened. One day I was at home resting and I decided to read one of them. I could feel her words lashing out at me from the paper. I ripped it up and threw it away immediately, along with the other letters. Maybe she'll figure it out one day. My life and sanity, has been so peaceful, not having to deal with her and Ron.

# 37

## COULD WEDDING BELLS REALLY BE IN THE AIR?

Jake continued to eat lunch at Jolynn's, but he never saw Charlotte again. Jake would leave Maggie generous tips and she would joke that if she kept serving him, she would soon be able to pay off her new car. Jake was starting to like Maggie and she liked him too. One day, on his lunch break, he asked her if she would like to see a movie the weekend and she agreed.

Friday afternoon, Jake arrived at Maggie's apartment around 7 p.m. Maggie had her hair up in a yellow-flowered headband and she had on a yellow sundress. Jake was accustomed to seeing her in her uniform and apron. She was beautiful, the wind raised her curly hair slightly - as she walked down the steps of her apartment. When she got in Jake's car, he loved the body oil that she was wearing. When he asked about her fragrance, she told him she had brought it from Jamaica.

Upon arriving at the theatre, they stood in line - waiting to purchase their tickets. It was as if they were the only two people there, they told jokes and laughed at each other. Maggie reached over to grab Jake's hand. It was a simple gesture, but it meant so much to him. Jake believed Maggie genuinely cared for him - with no strings attached. She didn't know how much money he had and neither did she care. While Maggie was talking, Jake looked over to the other line and he noticed Laverne standing there. She was with Paul Morgan, they had all went to school together. Jake couldn't help but notice Laverne was wearing a ring on her finger and appeared to be very happy. Maggie was still talking… but Jake was looking down at the floor, trying to process his thoughts. Jake had accepted his losses a long time ago, but he felt like he still owed Laverne a "Thank you and an apology." "They were up next to purchase their tickets, then he and Maggie walked over to get some popcorn and sodas. When they walked away from the concessions to find their seats, Laverne saw Jake out the corner of her eye. She was surprised to see him being such a gentleman, but she went on as if she never saw him.

About a year later, I was home on a Saturday afternoon, and I decided to check my answering machine. Jake had left a message saying... he and Maggie were getting married. I had to sit down for this one. I could not believe what I was hearing. They would be getting married in Jamaica, and he wanted me to be his best man. I thought I would see flying cows before I witnessed Jake getting married. Leave it to love to capture the hearts of those who have perfected the skill of masking past prey to manipulation.

I purchased my airplane tickets and cleared my work calendar for a week. I packed a lot of nice clothes, as I was expecting to have a good time on this trip apart from Jake and Maggie - after their wedding. When I arrived on the plane, I started putting my smaller luggage and bags in the overhead compartment. The flight attendant started complaining that all my bags left no room for the other guests to put their belongings. Before I realized it, I started becoming light-headed. I had to catch myself because I didn't want to cause a scene. Then I thought about Uncle Daniel again. I realized, it wasn't just the flight attendant, but it has been several women that I had encountered over the years... that made me lose my composure. Whether they were wrong or right, a simple confrontation makes me go from level 0-10 in a matter of seconds. I thought about the cashier at the grocery store last week, who claimed she accidentally overcharged me. After I confronted her about the items that she rang up twice on my receipt, I lost my temper before I could catch myself. I chose not to say anything else to the flight attendant for the rest of the flight.

Finally, we landed in Jamaica. I got checked into my hotel room, and then I went over to see Jake and the rest of the guys while Maggie was with her family. I didn't mention anything to Jake about how shocked I was that he was getting married. In fact, I liked the new Jake, and I didn't want to do or say anything to jinx his wedding. Ralph and a couple of Jake's cousins showed up later and we went to get something to eat. Jake wanted to make sure everybody had everything they needed for the wedding. When I got back to my room that night, I watched TV for a little while… as I anticipated the upcoming ceremony.

The next morning, Jake called to make sure I was awake. We had breakfast, then we all got dressed and drove over to the beach. Everything was already set up. What a beautiful sight. Maggie was gorgeous in her white lace, trimmed gown, and turquoise flowers in her hair. The maid of honor and bridesmaids wore turquoise dresses with white flowers on the side of their hair. Jake had on a black tuxedo with a turquoise tie and handkerchief, and so did the rest of the groomsmen. The ring that Jake had given me to hold for Maggie was beautiful. I knew he cared a lot for this woman. They looked good together too. This would be the first portrait Jake would take that Matt would not have to help him get dressed for. Speaking of Matt, I could not believe he was going to miss Jake's wedding, but we understood. Life is so unpredictable and complicated sometimes.

After the wedding, we celebrated. The next day I enjoyed some of the tourist attractions. This was a much-needed vacation for me. By the end of the week we returned to the States, and Maggie settled in with Jake. I think they are perfect for each other. Maggie doesn't praise Jake, she appreciates him, and he appreciates her. Maggie cooks American and Jamaican food, she keeps the house clean and does the laundry by choice, and not because Jake thinks that's what she is supposed to do.

As the years have continued to go by, Matt has become so attached to the church building. I believe he would be a perfect candidate for an intervention. When Jake and I leave our jobs in the afternoons, we go to our homes. When Matt leaves work, he goes to the church and stays there until late in the evening.

Sometimes, I receive phone calls for plumbing jobs in the Meadow Brook area. One afternoon, I drove by Matt's church and I saw him outside. It looked as if he had finished cutting the grass and was sweeping the debris off the porch and sidewalk. Matt appeared to have a million things on his mind, so I kept going. A month later, I saw his SUV at the church so I stopped to talk to him. He was cleaning the inside of the church. He appeared to recognize me at first, but then... he started preaching to me like I was a long-lost sinner who had never heard of the Bible in my life. I think he was still trying to prove that he was truly called by God. I placed my hand on his shoulder to get his attention, then I told him I just came by to visit and I would talk to him later. He stood there holding the mop and looking down at the kitchen floor...not saying a word...then he continued to mop. At one time, Jake and I thought it would be a shame for Matt to win so many souls and then lose his own to bitterness and unforgiveness, but now, we are more concerned about him losing his sanity.

As for myself, I don't know if I'll ever get married again... if I did, I would probably have to move to Jamaica. I don't want to have to go through the process of introducing anybody else to my family or explain the influx of letters and phone messages that I never respond to.

Well...today is the day. My first appointment with Dr. Weatherby. Getting out of my truck, I'm feeling anxious and perplexed about what will take place on the other side of that door. I figured... if I made the appointment, then that would give me the initiative to follow through with it. Walking towards his office door, I'm thinking to myself, I sure hope he can help me.